# DAYDREAMER

## Threads of the Forgotten
### Book 2 of the Daydreamer Saga

Rick Houghton

Table of Contents

*For the kind of love that would walk
through fire, bleed in silence,
and never ask to be named.*

## Content & Trigger Warnings

This work contains depictions of graphic violence
and themes of discrimination.

# CHAPTER ONE

## *I Give Upwards*

Hungary 1830

Mama says hunger makes a woman honest, but all it's ever made me is dangerous.

I chew on the thought as I adjust the strap across my shoulder. Five dead rabbits hang limp against my side, their warm bodies thumping with each step through the forest.

Dawn draws near, and already the ravens stir, cawing into the quiet. I've come deeper into the woods than I meant to, and the trek out is long. My legs ache, begging for rest— but the traders will open their stalls soon, and I need to be there if I'm to sell my catch. Devel knows we need the money.

This forest isn't like the last. It's denser here. We went

fourteen days without meat in that place. Fourteen nights of setting traps and stalking the woods before anything was caught. Hunger gnawed my insides raw, but nothing hurt like watching Maria waste away, colour drained from her cheeks, eyes dull with quiet pain. That was true suffering. But when hardship comes, I'm grateful to be Romani. Nobody suffers better than we do.

A raven shrieks above—louder now. The hush that follows is thick, unnatural, and cold.

And I feel it again—that strange flicker at the edge of my vision. Shadows bending unnaturally in the corner of my eye, and the scent of cold earth twisted with something darker—something not quite right.

I pause, breath hitching, heart thudding with warning.

Dati called my gift, *the sight*.

'Learn to control it, and you'll see what others cannot,' he said.

But he died before I could ever grasp it, and it seemed to die too. Until recently.

I take another step forward, and that's when I see it.

Something that doesn't belong. A scrap of deep red cloth snagged on a thorn. Not wool, not linen—something finer. Expensive.

I look around, but there's no path, no horse tracks. No one with fabric like that comes out this far.

Not unless they're running.

Or hunting.

And then I see something stranger still.

An unnatural shape juts from the bed of leaves like a stone stood on end. I peel a thorny branch from my leg and take a step closer, blinking through the half-light. It isn't a rock.

It's a boot—leather, upright, toe-first in the mulch.

I glance at the rabbits slung at my hip. 'What do you make of that?'

Their silence draws a dry chuckle from me.

Carefully, I descend the slope towards it, the first strands of dawn light casting strange shapes on the ground around me. I find a crooked branch and hook it by the laces, trying to lift it free from the swamp of leaves, but it doesn't move.

I set my traps down, grip the stick with both hands, and try again.

This time, the boot rises—dragging a leg up with it.

A cold weight drops in my chest. My fingers loosen before I can think, and the leg crumples back into the leaves, slack and heavy as death.

'*Mri Devla*,' I breathe—*my God*—voice unsteady, eyes lifting to the canopy above.

My heart thuds in my throat, heat rising through my skin. I slip the rabbits from my hip and set them on the ground. Then I inch forwards, knees brushing the cold earth, the stick trembling in my grip.

Carefully, I sweep the leaves aside—first with wood, then bare fingers.

A man's face stares up at me.

His skin is stretched thin over sharp bones, like he's been bled dry. His mouth hangs slack, lips peeled back from the teeth. Eyes, clouded and glassy, are fixed on the cracks of dawn bleeding overhead. A dark wound stains his temple, blood dried thick against his scalp. Maybe he stumbled drunk into the trees and struck his head. The gadje never could navigate the forest at night.

Strange that there is no smell. I know the stench of death, but all this man carries is the odour of the forest.

I clear a little more, and the truth reveals itself. His throat has been torn to shreds, but there's barely a drop of blood on the ground around him.

The stick slips from my hand. I turn aside, sucking in a shaky breath, and scoop a fistful of brittle leaves to cover the ruin as I gag.

'Devel,' I whisper through my fingers. 'What beast could do that to a man?'

After a moment, I steady myself.

I don't know who he is, or how to find his kin. But Dati wouldn't leave a man like this, and neither will I. A body should be buried or burned.

I glance back at my catch, then start gathering leaves by the armful, covering the man as best I can. Stones are scarce, but I find enough to build a modest cairn at his feet. I don't know any gadje prayers, so I whisper my own.

'*Dav opre.*'—I give upwards.

Shouldering my catch, I press on, deeper into my own thoughts. One day, this will all be behind me—the hunger, the pain, the struggle. Even hunting will fade into memory. A life lived and left behind.

The trees thin out ahead. I step into a patch of wet grass and mud, where rain has pooled beneath an old hornbeam tree. Something's churned up the earth into a slick puddle. A tangle of boar prints surrounds it—deep, round, rain-filled marks pressed into the dirt. The base of the tree is rubbed raw where it scratched.

The tracks lead into the thicket beyond, vanishing into the deeper dark, but the boar are long gone.

Behind me, a tall beech tree rises, bark smooth and grey, its branches well out of reach. I run my hand along the trunk, then press the blade of my knife to the bark and peel away a rough square. A clear mark. Easy to recognise. As I move through the forest, I carve one into a tree every two hundred steps. By the time I reach the edge of the wood, I'm certain I can find my way back to the boar's scratching post.

The trees give way to a bright morning sky, and the smell of campfires dampened by morning dew. Rudi stirs as I approach—short-haired, brown, and scrawny. He lopes across the grass to greet me, and I crouch to rub his head. Papa once said the Romani life ages you in dog years—seven times faster than most. The way my body aches, I think he might've been right. Devel only knows how old that makes this dog of ours.

Our tent is closest to the forest. Small and black, it shelters Maria and Luca when I'm away. Beside it sits my butchering block—oak, blood-stained and chipped. I unhook the rabbits and lay them down, then set to work.

Kneeling, I skin the rabbits. Rudi lies beside me, eyes fixed, waiting. He gets first pick of the feet before the rest of the dogs catch scent and come sniffing around.

I pour water into one of Luca's wooden bowls resting on the grass—rough, uneven, but a far cry from the splintered things he used to make in the weeks and months after his accident.

As I clean the blood from my hands, a sense of unease creeps over me. Wolves have been known to take down a man, but to leave him untouched?

The dogs snap at each other, fighting for scraps, and I fight down the image of the dead man and set about cleaning the furs.

Luca's decorative bowls are kept inside the tent, so they're the last thing I take before leaving for the markets. Three of them today—newly painted in deep blue and red, with black details curling along the rims. I tuck them into a satchel, sling the rabbits over my shoulder, and drape the hides across my arm.

Rain catches me by surprise, a light sprinkle on the dirt track as I leave camp, and it pulls me back to another place, another time in our lives.

A time Mama won't talk about. Everything that came before Dati's death is off limits to her. Too painful, I suppose.

By the time I reach the market, the sun is high and the sweat stings in my eyes.

'Hide ya purse,' a man calls across the street as I approach. Those on the opposites side laugh and glare as I trundle by. They lace their words with venom, their eyes too, but I am no stranger to either. All it takes is one honest trader, and we'll be fine for a few days and one step closer to leaving this life for good.

I pass a baker's stall, and my stomach twists at the nutty scent of warm bread. Saliva floods my mouth, and pain claws its way up from gut to throat. But I can't stop. Not yet. Not until I've offloaded the meat.

That's when I come to a butcher's stall.

A plucked duck hangs by its leg from the canopy above the stall. Pheasants hang by hooked beaks beside it. On the ground, caged hens squawk and flap, ready to be dispatched upon purchase.

I come to the front of the stall, wincing at the shrill squall. Half a lamb lays flat atop an oak slab, flanked by wicker baskets—one filled with trotters, the other with pig ears. Funny that there's no other pork on offer.

'What do you want?' The butcher steps out, wiping his

bloodied hands on a filthy apron.

'You don't have any rabbits,' I say, offering a smile as I bring my catch into view. 'Freshly caught and dressed. A top-quality butcher like you—'

'Why don't you tell me my fortune instead?' he cuts in. 'Got cards with you, or is it tea leaves you need?' He laughs, jowls quivering.

His words hit like a slap, but I force my jaw to stay loose, my smile fixed, despite the heat rising inside me.

'I'll sell for a fair price,' I say, voice easy, the way you speak to a skittish dog.

'Not fair enough.' He circles to my other side, reeking of blood, ale, and sweat.

My smile slips.

'Wouldn't trade with a filthy gypsy if you sucked my cock and threw the rabbits in for free.'

Something in me snaps—quick, cold. The knife's between his legs before I even think.

'Then maybe I'll take that little pecker of yours and use it to catch a fish. You like fish, gadjo?'

His face blanches. He stammers, words tumbling over themselves. 'Was only joking,' he stammers. 'A bit of banter. I love gypsies.'

'Then call me Romani.'

I shove him back and sheath the blade. 'Ignorant pig.'

He stumbles into the stall, and I walk on, calm on the outside, rage in my bones.

The fur trader's stall is quieter. She's foreign—an outsider like me. She takes the furs and the bowls at a fair price, though neither fetches much.

'Thank you,' I say, my eyes crawling over her inked hands and arms.

She shrinks back into the shadows, and I continue.

The next butcher's stall is bigger. Deer flesh hangs in thick slabs. Pigs and goats lay gutted across the counters. He already has rabbits, but they're scrawny. I scan the gloom and find the butcher watching me—round-bellied and broad, his eyes needle sharp.

'What do you want?' he says, laying a thick hand on the counter. He sniffs the air, as if he can taste my desperation. 'Selling or buying?'

'Selling,' I say. 'Five plump rabbits. At a good price.'

He nods at a basket of limp rabbits to his right. 'It'd have to be.'

I ease the weight from my shoulder and lay my catch between us. 'Freshly caught. Dressed clean.'

His eyes flick down. Back up. He grunts.

'Pheasant's what I need.'

'I don't have pheasant.'

'People got a taste for game birds. Bring me some pheasants, I'll pay fair.'

'You're not giving me a fair price now?' I lean in, forcing a smile. 'Stall like this—you must be rolling in it. I bet you could sell a beak to a duck.'

He chuckles, and I hate myself for it. Still, needs must.

We stand in a long silence—him, faintly amused; me, smiling through clenched teeth—until he slaps a thick hand on the counter, and I flinch.

'Half a gulden,' he says.

Relief floods me. 'Thank you.'

I wait for him to count the coins, breath caught in my throat. But instead, he places a single coin onto the counter and grabs the rabbits by their legs.

'Where's the rest?' I ask.

'Rest of what?'

'You owe me another two gulden.'

My voice is steady, but dread creeps in behind it.

'Half a gulden for the lot,' he says, softer now. 'Best I can do.'

I shake my head, staring him down, but I can't afford to lose my temper. Not here. Not now. Instead, I reach into his basket and take one of the scrawny rabbits, then pocket the coin.

'Bury me standing,' I mutter.

'What?'

'Nothing.'

I turn to go, but stop. 'What about boar? No one else in this market's got boar.'

He studies me for a moment. 'Stick to rabbits, little woman.'

'If I bring you a boar—will you pay what it's worth?'

'Better than anyone else would,' he says, turning his attention to a customer.

I move on, legs dragging, threading through the market chaos. Traders shout, customers push. I don't fight it. I'm too tired.

Sleep clouds my mind. My stomach twists, but the thought of eating that stringy rabbit turns it worse.

Then I remember the tracks.

Boar.

Real meat. Real coin.

It'll mean another night away from Maria and Luca. Maybe two. But it'd be worth it.

Maria comes barrelling up the track towards me as I come over the hill and down to the camp.

Warmth floods my chest, and I break into a run of my own.

When we're close, I sink to one knee, arms open, and she crashes into me for a hug. After a moment, I scoop her up, carrying her against my chest, kissing her cheeks as I walk.

She giggles and wriggles, telling me she missed me, and I hold her tighter.

'Mama, did you catch a rabbit?' she asks, reaching down to touch the small lapin hanging from my belt.

'Just a little one. We'll cook it with some carrots.' I kiss her again and set her down. She runs off, chasing Rudi through the tall grass, and I head for the tent—and Luca.

He limps into the blazing sun, masking his pain behind a smile as I approach. Then, he takes my hands in his.

'We missed you,' he says, pressing a kiss to my knuckles. 'I missed you.'

The look in his eyes is enough to warm me through, but my limbs are heavy. Yawning, I stroke his arm and sink to put my tools away in the tent.

He hovers at the entrance, lips pressed tight. 'You sold everything?'

I turn back, the weight of the day pressing down on me, and pull the coins from my pocket. I hold them out in my palm for him to see.

'I did.'

'Two gulden? For everything?' His shoulders sag.

I close my eyes and draw a slow breath before answering.

'They had plenty of rabbits already. I had to sell cheap.'

'And the bowls?'

How do I tell him the world doesn't value his bowls the way I do?

'Same really. More bowls than buyers.'

'So, what now?'

I glance over at Maria, laughing as she plays with the dog, and lower my voice.

'Take the money. Put it with the rest.'

I stand, lean in, and press a kiss to his lips as I slip the coins into his hand.

'Keep it safe, my love.'

Then I fetch the carrots from the bag beside the tent and make my way to the communal fire.

Mama stands as I approach, her face hard as coal.

'Here she is, the great huntress,' she calls. The other women turn to look, smirks tugging at their mouths.

'Behold the fruits of her labour. Meat for all.'

They giggle and sneer. I stop in front of her. I'm a head taller now, leaner too—but I see myself in her tired face.

'*Dosta,* Mama,' I say, taking her hand and urging her to sit. 'I do what I can.'

She sinks down onto a wooden stool by the fire, resumes plucking a hen, and I sit beside her.

'Family is the most important thing in this world, Nura. And you abandon yours in pursuit of what?' Her voice is rough as old rope. 'Give up these daydreams and accept your role in this community.'

Heat rises through me.

'And what role is that, Mama?'

'Men were not put on this earth to make bowls or raise children. Theirs is the burden of providing.'

'And what of those with husbands unable to provide?'

'The brothers and the father must provide if he cannot,'

croaks one of the elder women nearby.

'We can manage without his family.'

Mama sneers, eyeing the scrawny rabbit and limp carrots in my hand.

'With what? This?'

'It's enough.'

'This is not our way.' Mama clasps my hand, running her calloused thumb over my knuckles.

'Put your food with ours. Craft with us. Cook with us. Eat with us.'

'Mama, Luca is doing his best. I'll feed my family the way I know how.'

'We don't need charity. We need space'

'It is not charity, Nura. It is tradition. We are a community. We share. Did your dati teach you nothing?'

A bright rage flashes behind my eyes—but I force myself to think about tonight, about the boar, about the money that will buy our passage to a new life. And then the dead man slides into my thoughts.

'Mama,' I say, my anger turned cold. 'I saw something in the forest—a dead gadjo man.'

She continues to pluck the bird, sucking in a breath through her teeth. 'Another reason to stay out of there.'

The others cluck in agreement.

'Mama, his throat was torn open.' My voice cracks as I speak. 'He looked like he'd been bled dry.'

At this, she takes pause.

'*Mullo*,' someone whispers.

Mama rises and takes hold of my arm. 'Nura, there are strange things happening in those woods. If that man was killed by a *mullo*, then he will wake from the dead. Stay away, leave the monsters for those that hunt them.'

Everybody falls silent. All eyes fixed on me.

And I laugh—too loud, too long.

'Mama, you and your superstitions.'

I take the scrawny rabbit and the limp carrots, and return to our tent with a smile on my face, the word *mullo* in my ears.

When I return, Maria is still playing with Rudi. What I wouldn't give to spend the afternoon at play with her. But there's no time.

'Maria, come help me,' I call, taking the kettle from the tent and carrying it to our modest fire pit.

'But, I'm playing!'

My heart aches, but I keep my voice light.

'Come help your poor mama,' I say in mock sorrow. 'If you want to eat today, we need to get this fire up and the bunny cooking. Then I can get some rest before tonight.'

'Tonight?' Luca's voice cuts in, sharp with suspicion. He comes to sit by the pit with armfuls of dry wood. I pretend not to notice his stare as I joint the rabbit.

'What's tonight, Mama?' Maria asks.

I pause, wiping my hands on a rag as Luca adds wood to the fire.

'I found some markings in the forest. Boar. Tonight, I'll track them down and bring one home.' But as I look at Maria's bright eyes, a cold whisper edges through my thoughts and my mind coils around the torn red fabric in the forest.

'Gone again?'

My chest tightens. I twist a leg from the rabbit with unnecessary force.

'Baby, do you remember the plan we talked about?'

'Yes.'

I pull her close, lowering my voice. 'Remember, it's our secret. And we're close now, my angel. So close. But Mama has to do this last thing. I have to get a little more money before we can leave.'

'To England?' she breathes, her voice all wonder and hope.

'Shhh, darling,' Luca says quickly, gathering her to him.

'Remember, it's our secret. A new life.'

# CHAPTER TWO

## *The Cost of Survival*

I take Maria on a walk to the river. She runs, bounding through the grass, and I chase her down, my heart lightened by her laughter. She zigzags, evading me at every turn. When I catch her, I scoop her up and nibble her arms and tiny fingers.

She wriggles with uncontrolled laughter, and I carry her to the water's edge where I throw a small stone into the shallow stream, watching it skip twice before it sinks.

Maria copies me, her stone landing with a soft splosh just at the water's edge. I wish we could stay here forever, in this moment of simplicity, but the gnawing hunger in my belly and the ache in my legs remind me of the need to go back.

At the tent, I give Maria a book to read and ask Luca to watch her while I rest. My body aches for sleep, but my mind is restless.

I lie beneath my blanket, eyes wide open, imagining what life in England might be like—no longer an outcast, no longer a gypsy.

Sleep takes me eventually, but it's fitful. My dreams are filled with the forest and the dead gadjo. His pale face, eyes like sulphur.

I wake, drenched in sweat, my breath shallow and fast. I kick free of the blanket, wiping my brow with a cloth, but the chill lingers in my bones. It's as though something is reaching from beyond the dream world, fingers brushing against my skin. I rub my arm, where the sensation still clings, and scramble out of the tent.

The smell of stew grounds me. The sun has set, and the air has cooled. Maria sits with Luca, painting bowls beside a small fire, the scent of rabbit stew rising from the kettle suspended above the flames. When they hear my approach, both turn and smile.

'Mama,' Maria rushes to me, her small arms wrapping around me in a hug. 'Just in time.'

'For what?' I ask, grinning despite the lingering chill.

'Supper,' she says, pointing to the steaming kettle. Luca stands to embrace me, his long hair brushing my neck. I feel the strength in his arms, still there despite his injuries.

He ladles the stew into three plain wooden bowls and tears a hunk of bread into pieces. My stomach groans, urging me to eat.

'Where did you get fresh bread?' I ask, turning the crusty piece over in my hand.

Luca glances at Maria, then back at me, shifting his

weight just a touch. 'It was given to us.'

He spoons the stew into his mouth and drops his gaze to the bowl. I feel the weight of his silence.

'Who gave it to us?' I ask, setting the stew on the ground, my pulse quickening. 'Who gave us bread?'

'Does it matter?' Luca's voice is soft, like his eyes, but there's an edge to it now. 'We're hungry and they had bread to spare.'

'Am I not providing enough food?'

'Your mother just—' Luca begins, but I'm already up and moving towards the communal fire, ignoring his calls.

The pit is crowded tonight, but I see Mama sat with her back to me, drinking her tea. I arch my path to her so that I come up at her side. Sat beside her is Vaida, the eldest member of the community. They're deep in conversation with several other elders.

Mama looks up and sees me standing there, still clutching the bread. 'Good. You came.'

The elders turn to face me. I shake my head, confused.

'They didn't tell you?' she says, steam rising from the cup in her hands. Her voice is almost a whisper, but the look in her eyes is clear.

'Tell me what?' My breath catches.

'People have gone missing.'

'Who? What people?'

'From another community. They came to see us today.'

'I don't understand.'

'The gadje authorities are coming.' She shakes her head in disbelief. 'Rounding people up.'

'What are you talking about, Mama?'

Vaida looks up at me, his eyes like black pools of water. 'They want us gone from their land.' The gold rings on his fingers glint with firelight. 'We leave at dawn.'

'What?'

He rises to his feet, grey hair falling past his shoulders. 'They've passed a new law. Made it illegal to be Romani.'

'Who has?' My voice is thick, like I'm drowning in something heavy.

'The Gadje.' He brushes the hair from his eyes and looks into mine, his gaze unwavering. 'They've taken people already. Snatched away in the night.'

'It's not safe here anymore,' Mama cuts in.

I shake my head, trying to make sense of what I'm hearing. The words settle like a stone in my stomach as I think about the promise of a new life and how this affects it. 'They can't do that.'

'They have,' Vaida groans. 'We don't have time to argue about it. You are young and strong. You must help the others.'

I feel a knot form in my stomach. 'Vaida, I have a family of my own to take care of, and boar to hunt.'

'Boar?' Mama roars. 'You are no hunter, Nura. You're a mother. You must be ready to leave by dawn.'

'And what would leaving achieve?' I counter, my voice rising.

'Freedom.' Mama fixes me with a stony stare. 'Believe me, the pain of losing the ones you love is not to be taken lightly.'

'The next place will be no different.'

'Child, you are talking to your elders,' Mama snaps. 'Show some respect.'

I take a long breath and settle myself before speaking again. 'Vaida, I am sorry.'

'Good,' Mama says, her voice softer now. 'Now go and—'

'But I'm not leaving.' I fix my gaze on Mama, holding it there as long as I dare. 'This forest is plentiful. This forest has everything we need, and we are as safe here as anywhere else.'

Vaida sneers. 'You wear shame like a cloak, child. No food, no money, and no *Romanipen*. You long to be *Gadjikane*?'

His words hit hard, but I refuse to show it. I stand my ground, fists clenched.

Mama shakes her head, rising with her hands outstretched, but she's too late.

'You're right,' I say, trying to keep my voice level. 'I am full of shame. I'm ashamed that my family goes hungry and I'm ashamed that we're poor. And I don't want that for my daughter. I want to give her a different life.'

'You're ashamed to be Romani?' Mama asks, distress filling every crack of her face.

'No, never.' Tears fill my eyes and my stomach sinks. 'But I am ashamed of being a gypsy.'

I turn away before she can say another word, realising too late that I'm still clutching the bread. I toss it into the bushes, my heart heavy as I storm back towards the tent.


Both Luca and Maria have finished eating when I return. Maria looks up at me with brown swamps for eyes, and my heart aches. She's wrapped in a fur blanket that I traded for a doe many months ago.

'She wanted to have dinner with you,' Luca says in a gravelled tone. Leaning on his good leg, he takes my hand.

'Sit with us.' He pulls me down gently, and I pick up my bowl of stew to eat.

'It's so good. Did you make it?' I ask, leaning against

Maria's shoulder.

'I chopped the carrots,' she answers, smiling up at me, her eyes full of pride. I have to turn away to wipe mine.

'You did such a good job.' I say, kissing her cheek. She giggles, and I smile despite the churning worry in my gut.

'Did you read your book yet?' I ask.

'Baba said it's a gadje book,' she mumbles through a mouthful of bread. 'She'll bring me a proper book tomorrow.'

I brace myself for the hot swell of rage I know is coming, but I only feel deflated. A knife twists at the thought of Maria growing up as an outsider, as I have. As all Romani do.

'Baby, I'm sorry you're being told different things from different people. That must be confusing for you.'

I press her hand to my cheek. 'The book I brought you is a gadje book, yes. But it's also a brilliant book. One that will help you understand the world better.'

'Do the gadje know more about the world than we do, Mama?' she asks. 'Baba says we should stay away from anybody that's not Roma.'

I set down my bowl and pull Maria into my chest. 'When bad things happen, and when things get difficult, some people, including Baba, blame their problems, on others. But, in life, you must solve your own problems or they'll haunt you forever. Do you understand?'

Maria nods, her eyes full of innocent curiosity. 'I think so.'

I give her one last squeeze before standing and kissing her forehead. 'Time for bed, my angel. And it's time for me to head out.'

Luca takes Maria to the tent, and I finish the stew with Mama's words ringing in my ears.

When Luca returns, he takes my hands, his grip warm

and steady. 'You heard about the missing people?'

I nod. 'Mama told me.'

'I'm not sure it's the gadje.' He pauses to ensure Maria is out of earshot. 'They found three dead dogs—why would the authorities do that?'

'Who knows why they do anything?' I try to look assured. 'And you know how it goes. Probably one man and his dog got lost in the forest and they all add a little to the story until it's this big thing.'

'You're probably right,' Luca says. 'I left you something by the tent.'

I kiss him on the cheek, then stand to take a look.

Leaning against a wooden post is a short spear—oak with an iron head, strapped with leather and a copper crossbar. I pick it up and feel its weight in my hands. It's perfect.

'Where did you get this?' I ask.

Luca smiles, his eyes crinkling at the corners. 'Your dati gave it to me when we married. I always wondered why, but now I know he meant it for you.'

As soon as the words pass his lips, I recognise the spear. Luca has cleaned it, stained the wood, but it's unmistakable. 'Where's it been?'

'When he passed, I gave it to your mother.' His eyes shift to something distant. He looks at me in a way I haven't seen in years—the look he used to give when the drink had me.

'You weren't in a good place. Weren't interested in hunting. I thought any reminder of him might—'

'Thank you,' I interrupt, glancing over at Maria as she pops her head out of the tent.

She beams as I hold the spear up for her to see. It reaches only to my chest, but it's solid. Many boars have met their end with this weapon.

'Wasn't easy getting it back, mind.'

I chuckle. 'I bet.'

'That's not all,' Luca adds, his voice softening as he gestures to the back of the tent.

It takes a moment to register what Luca's showing me in the darkness. A trolley. He trundles over and pulls it forward. The wood is beautiful, meticulously crafted. A work of art. Handmade by my husband.

I kiss him, then take the handle of the trolley, pushing it back and forth. It's smooth, sturdy, and surprisingly light.

'I didn't know what I was making it for at the time.' He pauses, looks down at the trolley, then up to me. 'But it's perfect for a boar.'

It never occurred to me to need such a thing—Dati used to carry them across his shoulders—but I am not Dati.

I pull Luca into a hug and hold him tight. 'We're so close, my love,' I whisper.

'I know.'

'You don't think we should leave like everyone else?'

Luca takes a moment before responding. 'When I had my accident,' he says, his eyes flicking down to his twisted knee. 'That could have been the end of me. But you were so strong, so determined.'

I smile, remembering how he'd refused to leave the tent for weeks on end, and the satisfaction of finally getting him up and about.

'You can do anything, including hunting boar.' He looks deep into my eyes. 'And getting us to England.'

He hands me my hunting bag, smiles, turns and goes to the tent to check on Maria.

'Luca,' I call before he slips inside. 'You are my fire. *You* give me strength.'

He smiles, and I check the contents of my bag—cord, a flask, flint, a cloth, some nuts, and a map of the forest I made. Sliding my blade into its sheath on my belt, I set off into the night.

# CHAPTER THREE

*Boar and Blood*

I hide the trolley as near to the boar tracks as I can get it, glance up at the cloudless sky, and slip into the forest.

The undergrowth presses close around me, the darkness thick and unbroken. My thoughts drift—to the life I was promised when Luca and his dati came to arrange our marriage. They rode in from their community in a handsome cart drawn by two black drays, their legs thick as tree trunks—or so they seemed to me then. A show of wealth. I'll admit, I was taken in by it, feeling chosen, blessed. Devel knows I heard it often enough.

Scoundrels, Mama calls them now, and she's not wrong. Luca dislikes his family more than anyone. The irony is, I'm lucky to have him—though Mama would never say it. She'd send him back to his kin in a heartbeat if it wouldn't break Maria's heart — and mine. They were obliged to pay the bride price to Dati, but with Dati gone, Mama has no claim on that money. If I were in her shoes, I'd be angry too.

Through the creaking trees and the whine of insects, I catch the sound of something rummaging ahead.

Using Dati's spear for balance, I creep towards the noise. Heartbeat rising, I take a slow breath, reaching for the lessons Dati taught me — *breathe, listen to the forest, let everything else fall away.*

Focusing, I hear the creature scratching at the ground. I close my eyes, shutting out the noise of the forest, honing in. Too small. Too quiet. Not a boar.

I crouch low, moving cautiously, shifting my weight with each step. The bushes rustle. I glimpse the creature through the leaves and sink to one knee, raising the spear over my shoulder, free hand stretched forward. I throw.

The spear strikes something — a branch, not the target. A red fox bursts from the undergrowth, vanishing into the dark, no doubt chasing a mouse or some other small prey.

I curse, sharp with shame. If that had been real prey — or worse, a predator — I'd be dead or starving.

I retrieve the spear, cursing again as I wipe it clean.

As the adrenaline ebbs, the cold bites at my face and fingers. I rub my hands to bring the blood back and pause to eat a handful of nuts, scanning the trees. A small hazel catches my eye — green, flexible, exactly what I need.

I grip a branch and twist, working my way from tip to trunk, separating fibres until I can sheer it off with my knife. My palms burn, my wrists ache, but I keep going, twisting and slicing until I've gathered a small pile. I strip the fibres, weaving them into long cords, looping and securing them into circles, then hooking them over my shoulder.

If my map is right, I'm close to the boar tracks. And close to the dead gadjo.

I remember this part of the forest well—the ground sloping beneath the canopy, earth packed hard by centuries of shadow. Huge trees arch overhead, leaving space enough for an army to march unseen. I thought it then, and I think it now: this place is strange.

If Mama were here, she'd be telling tales of Baba Yaga and faeries. She'd say the trees move when you're not looking, twisting the paths to lead travellers astray. She'd warn me not to follow any lights between the trunks, no matter how sweet the music sounded. Not to eat, not to drink, not to listen. In these woods, she'd whisper—*even a prayer can turn against you*.

I smirk at the thought and spot one of my marked trees. I approach it, running my fingers over the bare patch of bark, imagining Dati at my side, whispering as he did when I was a child. He would take me into the woods to hunt, though I was hopeless—clumsy, giggling, scaring every creature for miles. He didn't mind. Devel, how I miss him. And Mama does too, though she'd never say it.

The path between the trunks narrows. Above, a sliver of starless sky appears, and the cool air brushes my face.

Then I hear it—a scream. Distant, unmistakable. It comes again and again, painful and haunting, setting off a chorus of sound: owls hooting, birds taking flight, frantic rustling in the trees.

My heart hammers against my ribs, each beat propelling me forward. My flesh burns with sweat. Another scream—sharper, higher-pitched.

Foxes, I tell myself. I've heard them a thousand times

before. But here, in this strange wood, the sound chills my bones.

I shift the spear to my left hand and draw my knife.

The clearing opens ahead—the place where the boars left their mark. Fresh tracks cut through the dirt. I crouch low, senses sharpening. I see more clearly in the darkness, hear more acutely.

The tracks lead in the same direction I'm heading. I follow, despite every instinct screaming at me to turn back.

To my right, a bank of rocks and dirt rises. I scramble up, find a flat spot, and slide the knife back into its sheath.

I hear the boar before I see it—big, black, grunting. The rumble of it thrums in my chest.

Sinking to one knee, I jam the butt of the spear into the ground, bracing it with all my strength.

The boar scents me. Snorting, sniffing, but without a flicker of fear.

I shift, just enough to let it see me. No going back now.

It scuffs the dirt, circling, snorting low —then charges.

I grip the spear with both hands, knee pressed into the earth, teeth gritted. I can't flinch. Can't turn away from the tusks bearing down on me.

At the last second, it veers, curving its charge.

I throw myself back, feeling the breath of it slick on my skin as the tusks slice past.

It barrels past, momentum carrying it down the slope. I draw my knife, ready, but it wheels around fast—too fast.

I thrust the blade into its neck. Blood wells, hot and thick, but the beast barely flinches.

I scramble to my feet and slide down the slope, dirt and stones tearing at my palms.

The boar crashes after me. Its bulk strikes with brutal

force, lifting me off my feet and slamming me to the ground. The impact knocks the breath from my lungs. My vision swims. Pain flares along my leg; blood soaks through my trousers.

No time to check it.

The boar is meters away, shaking its head, blood oozing from the wound at its neck.

It locks eyes with me.

It screeches—a raw, guttural sound. In its gaze, I see death.

I scramble up the slope, slipping and clawing my way to the spear. The boar charges again, its angry breath growing louder, closer.

I reach the spear, swing around it, and drop to my knees as I force the tip down into the beast's path.

The boar crashes into the spear, with the bladed end tearing into its chest.

The impact knocks me backward, but the beast keeps coming, screeching, blood and spittle spraying my face.

Flat on my back, I hold fast to the spear, praying it will hold.

The boar struggles, driving itself deeper and deeper onto the shaft, until it comes screeching up against the crossbar.

Devel, let the leather be good. Dati's voice echoes in my mind—plenty of men have died by speared boars when the bindings gave out.

I reach for my dropped knife but hesitate. I'm no fool. There's still fight in it. If I let my guard down, it'll rise again, wild as the reanimated beasts from Mama's tales.

I wait, blood burning against my cold skin, knife just beyond my grasp, one eye on the dying creature.

Slowly, the strength bleeds from it.

When it finally collapses, the silence crashes down so hard it stuns me. The world shrinks to the rasp of my own breath, the sting of sweat in my eyes, the thud of my heart finally slowing. My body trembles with the sudden absence of purpose.

I scramble back from the beast, peel open the seam of my trousers with shaking hands.

The gash on my shin is long but shallow; the flesh bruised but nothing broken. Or so I hope.

I tie the wound tight with a strip of cloth from my bag, blinking against the pain, each movement a reminder that I'm still alive.

Rolling onto my side, I find a position I can bear—and there, in the shadowed clearing, I watch the boar for a long time, the heat leaking out of it as surely as it leaks from my own body.

The patter of rain is what finally gets me off my arse. Every part of me throbs, but it's only when I try to stand that I learn what hurts the most. I howl and curse, hauling myself upright with the spear, my eyes locked on the boar, ready in case it springs to life.

Birds scatter as the rain thickens, and the sky darkens to slate. The packed dirt where I stand turns to a mud bath, and the slope becomes a stream of brown water—but the boar stays still.

I lay a hand on the beast's back and give thanks for its life. It's always strange, seeing something that was so full of power now lying so still. It pulls at the strings of my heart— until I think of Maria, and what this meat could mean for us.

Shivering, ignoring the pain in my leg, I set about freeing

the boar from the spear. I shove with my shoulder, pull at its hind legs, but it won't budge. The only way is to dig the spear out of the earth with my bare hands and my knife. By the time I'm done, I can't feel my fingers, but there's no time to stop. Not here.

I've gouged a trench behind the spear, and bracing myself in a squat, I wrench the shaft upwards. The boar drops with a wet thud, and I'm sent tumbling back down the slope. For a moment, I imagine myself bloodied and alone beneath a pile of leaves.

Getting the boar onto its back drains the last of my strength. There's no dragging him out of here like this. I close my eyes for a moment, searching my memory for Dati's old lessons. What to do, and in what order?

I wipe the knife clean against its fur and get to work, opening him up from pelvis to throat, using my fingers to lift skin away from guts. The spear's path tells its story—heart pierced, lung nicked, stomach nearly ruptured.

Nicking away any sinew holding things in place, I scoop the heart, lungs, and stomach back towards the hind, and haul out the guts in one steaming, heavy mass—maybe a quarter of the beast, dumped into the mud.

Next comes the part I always hated—the head has to come off. No sense hauling dead weight.

My knife slices easily through the thick flesh of the neck, but separating the spine takes work. I twist and wrench until it cracks. The stench rises, curling into my throat like a fist. I gag, steady myself, and think of what's at stake.

A beast this size should fetch enough that we can finally pay for our passage out of here. Not in comfort, but comfort's a luxury we can live without.

I take the plaited hazel cord and loop it around the hog's

ankle, fastening the ends with a friction knot. I braid any loose fibres together to make a rough handle.

Soaked to the bone and gasping for breath, I lean on the spear and set off, dragging the heavy bastard out of the woods, blood and bile thick in my mouth.

Through forest detritus, I use raw and bleeding hands to roll the beast over roots and branches, but it's slow going, especially with Dati's spear. I need both hands to haul the boar. My lungs burn, leg throbs, the damned beast is slick with rain.

I need to take the shortest path out of the woods, even if it means passing by the dead gadjo. The going will be easier on open ground.

But the thought stirs something in my stomach. A flutter that grows into clawing unease as the cairn comes into view —half toppled.

I don't have time to waste—but still, I pause.

I leave the sodden boar in the mud and pick up a flat stone, wiping it clean on my trousers. Dropping into a squat, I place it gently on the cairn.

But something's wrong.

My stomach flips. I stagger backwards.

The gadjo is gone, and in his place the ground is scorched. Leaves turned to ash.

A chill slides over my skin.

'Devel,' I whisper. Was mama right about this place?

The forest seems to shudder. My vision blurs. My skin prickles.

I have to get out of here—now.

But I have to choose: Dati's spear or the boar. I can't carry both.

The past or the future.

I crouch low, the spear across my lap, my hands running along the worn shaft while my eyes scan the shifting shadows. I've been lost since Dati died—adrift, and unable to find my way back. But now, for the first time, I can see the light, see a way out of the darkness. And I know what he would tell me—he'd want this for me, for Maria. He'd understand better than anyone the cost of survival.

'I miss you,' I whisper before jamming the spear into the wet ground. Tears spill, sharp as splinters, and my chest feels ready to crack. I touch my fingertips to the spear one last time and swallow down the lump in my throat.

A hush falls over the forest, and there's just my heartbeat and the whisper of wind over the treetops.

'You gave me this to hunt. Now I leave it in peace. *Sastimos ta Devlesa,* Dati.'—*Health and go with God.*

I take one last look before setting off again. Every muscle burns, begging me to stop. The drizzling rain needling against my skin.

Eventually, the rain eases. The trees thin. Beyond the forest, daylight spills over a boggy field, and the ground—though slick—makes dragging the boar a little easier.
I slip and slide, falling face-first into the mud with a wet slap, but I'm making progress, and that's what matters.

I've strayed far from where I first entered the woods, so I follow the treeline until the land feels familiar beneath my boots.

There, half-sunk into the muck, I find the wooden trolley.

I drop the boar beside it and double over, dragging in great heaving breaths.

Blood runs from my hands to my wrists, but it's nothing compared to the agony that stabs through my shin the moment I stop.

I peel back the split trouser leg. Blood has soaked through the cloth bandage, darkening my boot to a deep, wet red.

I'm not the squeamish sort, but the sight leaves me dizzy. I sink onto my other knee, stay there until the spinning eases.

And while I crouch in the cold mud, my mind fills with questions about the dead gadjo—and the charred earth left in his place.

A shudder crawls up my spine. The cold finds its way beneath my clothes, burrowing into my bones.

But then I remember one step that I've missed. One that Dati would be screaming at me for skipping.

'Skin the bastard,' I mutter to myself. 'Before it spoils.'

Starting at the cleft of the hoof, I cut up along the leg to the shoulder, nicking at the fat and flesh as I peel back the hide.

I work my way down, from the back leg to the front. Then down the inside of the foreleg, tugging the skin free as I go.

My hands ache from the effort. Boar hair lodges in the open wounds on my palms.

I grip the thick fur at the belly, squat low, and heave with everything I have left. The beast rolls onto its front with a wet, sucking sound.

I pull the hide from the back towards the neck, slicing away the stubborn pieces until, at last, it comes free in a heavy, sodden sheet.

It's hard to get moving again.

But I force myself to drag the trolley a little further. One step. Another. Each one drags me closer to the life we need.

Mud clings to my boots, the boar's weight pulls at my arms, but inside me a flutter of excitement stirs—small at first, then stronger with each step.

Hours slip past. The sky stays low and grey, pressing against the earth.

And then, at last, I catch the scent of smoke and roasting meat.

Hear the distant clatter of carts and voices.

The market.

If I could run, I would.

My legs are spent. My body broken.

But my heart has already raced ahead.

# CHAPTER FOUR

*Leaning on the Past*

The rain has stopped, but there's no sign of the sun. Throngs of people shuffle up and down the cobbled path, like a wall meant to keep me out. Their haggling and banter an indecipherable din. The heavy, sweet stench of perfume and sweat almost unbearable.

They shift when I near, like waves parting for a rock— glaring, whispering. They cling to their valuables, eyes sharp and watchful.

I keep my head down, focused on the pain as I drag the heavy cart to the butcher's stall.

The butcher stands a head taller than any man I've ever seen—tall enough to see me coming through the crowd. He wipes his hands down his bloodied apron, swipes at a cluster of buzzing flies, and steps forward to inspect the boar.

'Big bastard, ain't he?' He takes hold of the boar's leg and lifts it up for a quick look underneath, then lays it back on the trolley. 'Didn't think you had it in you.'

'Sixteen gulden,' I tell him.

He laughs. Big, booming chuckles that resonate in my chest.

'A month's wages, that is.' He takes the cart from me and wheels it to the stall. 'I'll give you eight.'

I tighten my grip on the handle, wincing as pain flares through my hand. 'Fourteen.'

'Ten.' He bends over for another look, then straightens to meet my eyes. 'Best offer.'

Passersby glance our way, frowning. It wouldn't do for his business to be seen trading too easily with someone like me. I can't afford to be forceful, but this sale means everything. Get it right, and I'll never need to hunt again. I can't afford any more setbacks.

'Be fair. I have a daughter.' I try to give him a kind look, though I'm not sure if it shows. 'Twelve gulden—and we can both eat tonight.'

He studies me for a few beats, then nods. He fishes into his purse and hands me the coins.

'Bring the head next time.'

'There won't be a next time.' I slip the coins into my pouch. 'What about the trolley? It's yours for two gulden.'

He looks the trolley over and slips me another four gulden without a word. I take it with a disgruntled huff and start for the fur trader's stall, bitter at always being on the losing end of these negotiations.

It's all I can do not to lash out at the first gadjo who

stares too long when I pass him again. But I calm myself by thinking of how close we are to leaving this all behind.

'You're a very capable woman,' the fur trader says as I approach.

It takes a moment to spot her at the back of her stall, hidden amongst the shadows.

'It took a great deal more effort for me to garner any respect from these milk-skinned men.'

'I don't hear any insults thrown your way,' I say, leaning against her counter, squinting into the darkness. 'When they catch sight of my face, their eyes fill with anger like I've wronged them personally.'

She comes forward into the light with a grace that reminds me of the princesses in Maria's books, a thick rope of plaited black hair swinging behind her, a red dot glistening on her forehead like a drop of blood.

'They don't like you. But not because you are a gypsy. Because you are strong,' she says, her accent thick.

'Don't call me that,' I snap.

She smiles, the light falling across her face. Though her features are smooth, there's a hardness beneath them.

'My words cannot hurt you.'

I lift the boar hide for her inspection, but she doesn't look at it. Her gaze pins me instead, sharp and assessing.

'It must be difficult,' she says, 'for such a beast to accept death from something as beautiful as you.'

Heat creeps up my neck. I hold her stare as long as I can, then glance away.

'How long have you been here?' I ask.

My sudden change of topic amuses her. A smile feathers across her face. 'Too long.'

She rounds the counter and lifts the hide from my arms.

'Far too long,' she says, her gentle tone cracking.

She spreads the hide across her table, running her hands over the fur. Rings flash on her fingers—silver, bronze—but one catches my eye: a gold band crowned with a blood-red stone, glowing as if it were warm with life.

'This is good work,' she says, lifting her head to look at me. 'You're skilled with a knife. But you must be careful. There are things in this forest you would not wish to meet.'

The dead gadjo flashes into my mind, ice-cold fingers clawing at my spine.

'I can look after myself,' I mutter.

'I can see that,' she says, big brown eyes studying me.

Three, four breaths pass. I want to look away—almost do —but something in her gaze roots me to the spot.

Finally, her eyes drop. 'You are a rare one.'

'One of a kind,' I say, a sudden tiredness coming over me.

'Beautiful yet fierce,' she says. 'Tell me — do you believe in reincarnation?'

It's hard not to shift my feet, to glance away.

'You sound like my mama,' I say.

She lets out a small laugh and turns back to the boar skin.

'I'll take him,' she says, disappearing into the back of her stall. She returns with a small drawstring bag and presses it into my hand, heavy enough to almost slip through my fingers.

'Payment for the fur,' she says, 'and a little something extra — to keep you away from the forest.'

I weigh the bag in my palm. It's far more than the butcher paid for the meat.

'This is too much,' I say.

'No, it isn't.'

A laugh bubbles up from my chest, surprising even me.

'This will change our lives,' I whisper.

'Then it is definitely not too much.'

She slips back into the shadows, her amber-coloured dress sweeping behind her.

'Be safe,' she calls.

'Tell me your name!'

'Aisha,' she says from the darkness. 'Though I expect you'll never need it.'

'I guess not,' I say, smiling as I clutch the bag of coins tight against my chest. 'Thank you, Aisha.'

I turn for home, wincing as the pain flares again in my leg.

'Wait,' Aisha calls out. 'You're hurt.'

I look down at my blood-filled boot, then turn back to her stall as she steps out into the light.

The man in the next stall glares at me, his eyes fixed on my bloody leg.

'Savage,' he mutters as I limp past.

'Let me see,' Aisha says, falling to her knees before me. She gestures for me to loosen the cloth tied around my shin.

I obey, though my fingers are clumsy. When the cloth falls away, the gash is worse than I thought. The sight of it makes the world tilt and dim.

'Come,' she says, drawing me back into the cover of her stall. She eases me onto a wooden stool and pours water from a canister onto a cloth, then begins washing the wound.

I wince at the pain, teeth gritted, light pulsing at the edges of my vision.

When she wrings out the cloth, her hands run red with my blood.

'You're lucky,' she says, glancing up at me with soft

brown eyes. 'Many men have bled to death, courtesy of a boar's tusk.'

'Thank Devel I am no man, then,' I mutter, hiding the tremor in my voice.

She smiles at that, then slips back into the shadows.

When she returns, she's holding a wooden cane—beautifully carved with ghouls and flames, the handle fashioned into the image of a skull.

'It belonged to a friend of mine,' she says, offering it to me. 'You'll need to return it before you leave for your new life.'

I run my hand over the carvings, feeling every groove, every detail. Immediately, my mind flickers to Dati's spear—lost, abandoned in the woods—and my stomach tightens with guilt.

'I have to go,' I cry out, the weight of Dati's abandoned spear knotting in my chest.

Aisha's gaze sharpens.

'I mean, thank you, but my family is waiting.'

I rise unsteadily and try to hand the cane back to her.

'I can't take this.'

She steps back, refusing it.

'You cannot walk,' she says firmly. 'Take the cane. Heal. Return it to me when you're ready to leave this place behind.'

I look at it again, unease prickling along my spine.

'I can't bring this home,' I say. 'It's decorated with *prikaza* —bad omens.'

At that, Aisha smiles, and with a slow grace, she rolls up her sleeves.

In the dimness, it's hard to make out what she is showing me, but then my mind pieces together the tattoos of monsters and ghouls, devils wreathed in fire, inked boldly along her arms.

'We carry them with us,' she says, voice soft and sure, 'to show there is nothing to fear.'

In her flowing dress, it would be easy to mistake Aisha for something delicate. But beneath, I can see that she masks a fierce strength.

'Who are you?' I ask.

'I'm Aisha, the fur trader,' she says with a light smile.

'Who are you really?'

She leans closer, takes my blood-smeared hands in hers, and looks deep into my eyes.

'Who are you really?' she echoes. 'A Romani mother? A hunter? A would-be gadjo?' Her grip tightens when I try to pull away.

'We are all a mystery, even to ourselves.'

She lets go, and I rock back, heart pounding. 'I am no gadjo.'

'Go home to your family,' she says. 'Celebrate your success. Heal.'

She presses the cane firmly into my hand and turns her back on me before I can argue.

'Take it.' She turns her back before I can argue, her shadow lengthening like a veil behind her.


I set off, doing my best to hide the pain in my leg and refusing to lean on the cane.

I'm sure Aisha is watching, amused, as I teeter along—but I keep my head high and my teeth clenched until I'm out of sight.

Only once I leave the market behind and reach the open road do I let the pain escape, grunting and cursing under my breath.

The cane, despite everything, proves to be a blessing. Still, I must not let Mama see it.

The journey is slow—slower than I'd like. The hills are worse than ever, and oddly, the descents are harder than the climbs.

But finally, I reach the last crest and see the gravel track winding down into the camp.

And I stop dead.

The camp is gone.

At first, I think I've made a mistake—that I've taken a wrong turn, that I'm looking in the wrong place.

But no. That's our tent. That's our fire pit. And everything else... is gone.

No smoke rises. No dogs bark. No voices call out.

The world below is still and empty.

A cold fist clenches around my heart.

Mama left us. She took the others and left.

The pain of that thought flashes through me—but then fury chases it away.

Fine. Forget Mama. We have the money now. Luca, Maria, and I can start our new life—away from this place. Away from her.

Energy surges through me. If I could run, I would.

At least now, there's no need to hide the cane.

I hobble down the track, heart pounding with anticipation.

Any second now, Maria will spot me and come rushing up the path.

I ache for it. I miss her every night I'm away—but that life is over now. Over.

Strange, though... no one's up and about. At this hour,

they should be crafting, cooking, playing.

Still, I reach the tent, prodding the canvas with the cane, the grin fixed on my face.

I shake it once, then again, waiting for a voice, a giggle—anything.

Nothing.

I duck down and peer inside.

The mess hits me first—blankets tossed aside, clothes abandoned on the ground. Maria's wooden doll lies face-down and forgotten. The sight of it now rolls my stomach.

They aren't here.

But they wouldn't leave with Mama.

They *can't* have.

The air seems to vanish from my lungs. I double over, gasping, my thoughts spiralling.

Where would they go? Why would they go?

I clutch at the edge of the tent, shaking.

Then the shaking turns to weakness. My body won't hold me. Every muscle thrums with exhaustion, heavy as stone. I crawl inside and pull the furs over me.

*They can't be far,* I tell myself. *They'll be back soon.*

And I fall into a deep, aching sleep.

Sometime later, I wake with a jolt, disoriented. The pain in my leg and back reminds me where I am.

There's movement outside—soft shuffling, the rustle of leaves. I smell smoke.

They're back. They're being quiet so they don't wake me.

My heart leaps.

I scramble out of the tent, only to find Rudi, the old mongrel, nosing curiously at the cane.

Night has fallen. The air smells of smoke and damp earth. The cold bites at my skin.

I turn in a slow circle, searching the empty camp.

There's no one.

No Luca.

No Maria.

No Mama.

Only me, the dog, and the cold.

The weight of it crushes me, stealing the breath from my lungs.

I collapse into the dirt, a thousand wild, terrible thoughts battering at my mind.

And still, the dark stays silent as the dead.

# CHAPTER FIVE

## *Where Shadows Take Them*

I sit stewing in the anguish of it all.

Have they left me behind?

Or were they taken?

I don't know what it means.

Why would Luca leave me like this?

The thought creeps in—maybe he's tired of my ways. Maybe he *does* want to raise Maria in the Romani way, and I've been too stubborn to see it.

Too stubborn to listen.

*Devel.* Why am I always so bad at listening?

What if I never see her again?

Before I realise it, I'm on my feet, pacing. Rudi trots at my heels, anxious.

A wave of nausea folds me over. A cramp seizes my gut so tight I can't breathe. My heart feels ready to burst through my ribs and scatter me in pieces.

I can't take this.

And then—Dati's voice, low and calm, cuts through the storm in my head.

*Slow down*, he used to say. *Take a moment. Think about the next move. See what's coming. Plot your course.*

I sink to my knees. Eyes shut. Hands trembling.

I drag in lungfuls of cool night air. Hold it until my chest burns. Force my mind to focus. *Why?*

Why would Luca leave me?

Why would he take Maria from her mama?

The answers are the same—he wouldn't. Not unless someone made him.

The thought of Maria, ripped from this place without me, twists something deep in my chest.

She must be terrified, hurting—and for what?

So I could prove I'm strong enough to take down a boar?

I bite my lip until it bleeds. My fists clench.

The bloodstained butcher block looms nearby, abandoned.

I turn on it, punching again and again until my knuckles split—until the sting in my hands matches the one behind my eyes.

My thoughts spin.

Were they taken by the gadje?

Taken by Mama?

Or did they go looking for me—and now they're lost in the woods?

Dread seizes my body. Blood rushes in my ears. I lurch to my feet.

Rudi jumps up beside me, eager to help. I snap, shoving him away.

'Fucking mutt. You're supposed to protect them.'

He looks up at me with those soft brown eyes. The venom drains from my voice.

'Sorry,' I mumble, reaching down to scruff his head.

But the image won't leave me—Maria, out there. Alone. In the dark.

My heart hammers again.

Mama's tales of witches and fae were always just that—stories.
Folklore.

And yet...

I saw something in those woods.

More than saw it—*felt* it.

Something strange.

Something real.

Flushed with fear, I snatch up my blade and charge towards the treeline—and the darkness beyond.

But what if they're not in there?

What if they come back—and I'm the one who's gone?

I skid to a halt just shy of the trees, torn.

Rudi watches me from where he sits, unmoving, eyes wide.

Of all the thoughts spiralling through my head, one keeps circling back: *Mama*. She warned me they'd leave.

Why didn't it occur to me she might make them go?

She's always tried to control me—this would just be her latest trick. Another way to bind me to the camp: stealing the ones I love. It fits perfectly with Mama's tinctured, twisted view of the world.

Fury rises in me, fast and fierce, like fire through dry wood.

This will be the last time she sees Luca or Maria.

The way I feel right now, it might be the last time she sees *anyone.*

I turn on my heel and head for the path out of camp, strapping my knife to my belt.

Then I remember the money.

Cursing, I duck back into the tent and claw through the mess, fingers scrambling for the drawstring bag. On the way out, I grab my hatchet too—who knows how much support Mama has from the others.

No matter. I'm taking my family back—whatever it takes.

Halfway up the track, I stop again, chest heaving. My jaw aches from how tightly I've been clenching it.

I glance back.

Rudi still hasn't moved.

What does he know that I don't?

A sudden thirst scrapes my throat raw. I yank my bag around and dig for the flask. When I can't find it, frustration boils over. I dump the whole thing out, scattering everything into the dirt.

'Fuck's sake,' I shout, stamping the ground like a child.

The flask rolls free at last, but by then, I've half-ruined what little order I had.

I take a long pull. The water clears a path down my throat. Tears slip hot down my cheeks.

I kick my scattered belongings into the grass. I hate myself for being this uncertain. This lost.

I pace the path like a caged animal, thoughts chasing each other in circles.

Finally, a decision forms.

I'll wait out the night.

But waiting *here* will drive me mad—and sleep is out of

the question.

So I'll walk. Just for a while.

I leave the hatchet and knife, then scrawl a note, quick and messy: *Don't go anywhere. Be back soon.*

I pin it to the tent flap where any returning eye will catch it, then set off along the path into the town.

This time, Rudi follows without hesitation.

The town rises ahead, the church spire stabbing the night sky like a threat.

As we draw near, I see a crucifix mounted on a post outside the church, a steepled wooden roof above.

The tortured son of God hangs there, naked but for the splintered loincloth and the battered roof.

Paint has peeled from his face in curling flakes. His wooden fingers are rotted to the bone.

And still—there's comfort in his ruin.

I've never been much for religion, but tonight, seeing him like this—scarred, forgotten, suffering—*but unbroken*—it gives me hope. Draws me in.


I stand before Jesus, unsure if I should venture inside, when something else catches my eye—a tavern. The kind of place I used to vanish into after Dati died. The kind of place Luca would have to drag me out of.

'The Fox and the Hound,' I whisper, reading the painted sign.

The door is black as soot, set into a pale stone wall. I push through, expecting the hum of drinkers and clatter of mugs.

Instead, I'm met with a stairwell plunging into darkness.

I hesitate at the top, a prickle of unease crawling up my spine. Luca's face flickers across my thoughts.

The sour-sweet scent of ale drifts up, carrying the

promise of sweat, smoke, and old regrets. My stomach knots the further I descend. I try to shake Luca's voice from my head, to pretend I don't feel his judgement clinging to me like cobwebs—but it's there, and I've never needed a drink more.

At the bottom, another door waits, fitted with a brass handle. I should turn and go back up the steps. Only trouble lies beyond this door.

I pull my hood low, glance down at Rudi, and open it.

Warmth hits first. Then noise. The tavern is carved into stone, dimly lit, its pillars damp and moss streaked. Laughter and shouting echo off the walls. People crowd every nook and alcove. I try to close the door softly, but it thuds behind me—no slipping in unseen.

Keeping my head down, I search for a place to sit and spot an empty table tucked into a shadowed corner. Rudi curls beneath it as if he knows the place. I wait, half-expecting to be thrown out, but the innkeeper ambles over with a tankard already in hand.

I slide a coin across the table. He says nothing—just sets the drink down and turns away. Gaunt and stooped, he's too tall for this underground world of his.

I catch a wisp of conversation, something about a missing family, but when I try to listen, the conversation fades into the background.

Did I imagine it?

I take a long look at the drink before me, pushing back the urge—the need—to drink. But it's no use.

One swig, and I'm back in the days—the weeks and months—after Dati died. Back when ale and wine were the only things that dulled the pain. And the fastest way to enrage Mama.

The cup is empty before I realise it. I should leave. I mean to. But as the innkeeper passes, he pauses beside my table.

'Another?'

I nod before I can stop myself. He takes the empty tankard, and I brace to stand—but I'm still sitting when he returns with the next.

My hand shakes as I lift the drink. I drain half in one go. Only then do Dati and Luca fade from my thoughts, just long enough for another name to rise.

'Maria,' I whisper into the cup.

The drinks keep coming. I keep drinking. I spiral through fear, to grief, to fury. The heat of it creeps up my neck, burns beneath my skin—but each cup snuffs the flames a little more, until I'm drenched in self-pity and barely upright.

When the innkeeper passes again, I lurch forward and grab his arm. 'My family is missing,' I say. 'I need help.'

He looks around, then comes closer. 'Ain't nobody here gonna help you. Best keep your voice down.'

'Someone has to know something,' I spit.

The tavern's roar dims without warning. Rudi stirs, a low snarl curling in his throat.

I clutch the table, brace to stand—just as a figure approaches through the gloom.

'She's a gypsy,' he grunts, stepping closer.

Rudi rises, shoulders low, hackles raised.

I lift my gaze to meet the bearded face glowering down at me.

'Her family's missing,' the innkeeper says.

'Piss off,' the man tells the innkeeper without taking his eyes off me.

Then he leans in. 'Bout time they cleared you lot out. Bring bad luck, you do.'

I try to rise, but the world fuzzes, legs feel unsure.

'Leave her be,' the innkeeper calls. 'She's a paying customer, just like you.'

'We've got missing of our own, and I reckon you lot are to blame.'

He reaches for my hood, but Rudi lunges with a bark. The man stumbles back—not bitten, but rattled.

'Don't fucking touch me,' I hiss, rising to my feet. The tremor in my hand is gone. The whole tavern falls silent, save for Rudi's growl.

'We'll leave. I don't want any trouble. But don't ever touch me.'

For a moment, no one moves. I reach down to signal Rudi —and then the man lets out a hoarse laugh.

He saunters to the bar, snatches a cup from the innkeeper's hand, downs it, and slams it on the counter. Foam clings to his beard as he wipes his mouth.

'She's payin' for that one,' he says with a crooked grin.

'Fucking gadjo,' I mutter, too quick for sense to catch up.

But he hears it.

'You should watch that mouth of yours if you don't want trouble.'

He spins. Lunges at me with his thick butcher's hands and hurls me out of the corner and across the room. I hit the wet floor hard—and Rudi's jaws are already sinking into his thigh.

'Get the dog,' someone shouts. Four men pile in. I twist to see them wrench Rudi away and hurl him through the stairwell door. It slams shut behind him. His barks and scratches echo in the stone.

Then they turn on me.

I scramble up, but a boot finds my ribs. White-hot pain blinds me.

'Gypsy witch,' someone yells.

Another kick comes, but I roll aside just in time. Laughter now. Jeering.

I crawl behind a pillar, use it for cover, drag myself upright. My side screaming, my head swimming. I step out — and the bearded man swings a punch.

I slip past it. Grab his arm. Slam it against the stone. My knee drives into his thigh — he buckles — and I smash my elbow into his eye.

He staggers back, stunned.

He doesn't realise I've been fighting boys like him my entire life.

I'd almost enjoy this — if I weren't underground, alone, and surrounded by pigs.

I hold his glare and see exactly what the big gadjo's thinking. If we were alone, he'd walk away. But we're not. So, he has to perform. He clomps forward, fists raised — and quick as a mule, I stamp my foot into his front knee.

It doesn't break, but it buckles. He knows now to keep his distance.

But there's only one way I can win this: get him on the ground. But not here. Not with this pack of pigs ready to pile on the moment I gain the upper hand. I need another way.

He circles right. I match him, and I see the chance I need. A few more steps and I'll be at the door. I'll bolt up the stairs and be gone before these fat bastards can even jam themselves through the frame.

Just a few more steps.

He lunges with a growl. I duck his fist, slip aside. The door's close — close enough to reach in a single dash. If it were just the two of us, I'd go for it. But I hesitate. One second too long.

Hands grab me from behind.

My arms are yanked back, twisted.

'You never should have come down here.'

I twist, I kick—but then the first prick, the bearded one, slams his fist into my jaw.

Everything goes white.

I hit the floor.

They haul me up again. Blood fills my mouth. I spit a tooth.

Another punch. This time to my ribs—the same spot they kicked before. I scream. Tears come, unbidden and hot. I hate that they've dragged this out of me, but I can't stop it now.

Then it's just pain. Blows, one after the other—crunching bone, flashing light, iron in my mouth.

And then I'm weightless.

They carry me out like a dead dog.

At the door, Rudi's growl makes them pause—until a heavy blow cuts him off mid-snarl. A yelp.

Then cold.

The street.

They toss me into the night like garbage.

Someone mutters something about gypsies, but I'm past hearing.

Boots crunch away into the dark. The door groans shut behind them.

I lie there, head ringing, ribs shattered, face burning with blood and shame and swelling.

Rudi finds me. Licks my hand.

I'm so stupid.

So. Fucking. Weak.

I swore last time this would never happen again.

But here I am.

Ears ringing, head throbbing.

I close my eyes and drift.

Back to the woods. Back to Dati.

He's kneeling over the steaming carcass of a fallow deer, peeling back the skin with long, clean strokes. Blood runs from fingertip to elbow, speckling the snow. The smell of iron and pine cling to the air. Dati's breath smoking like a furnace as he works.

'Pay close attention,' he snaps, flecks of claret flying from his hand. 'You'll do the next one.'

I shuffle closer on my knees, the cold biting at my skin.

'None of the other kids have to hunt.'

He glances sideways at me, hands still moving, smooth as silk.

'What I want for you isn't what their datis want for them.'

I wake, confused and aching. The dream slips away like smoke. I wipe my face and sit up, every movement dragging pain behind it. It takes a moment to register—my rings are gone. I lift my hands, staring at the bare fingers like they belong to someone else. Consequences. Stupid, stupid girl.

The tavern door crashes open. Two drunken louts stumble out, voices loud with laughter. I don't wait. I drag myself upright, jaw clenched, ribs on fire, and hobble off just as one swings a boot that grazes my backside.

'Gypsy filth.'

My head pounds, my jaw throbs, ribs grating with every breath as I make my way down the uneven streets, Rudi limping by my side. Each step pools more dread in my stomach, rising like floodwater. But somewhere deep in the ache and shame, a moth stirs—its wings hope, its flight desperate optimism. Maria and Luca must be back by now. They'll be waiting.

We can leave this godforsaken place.

I stop and lean against a stone wall, spitting blood into the dirt. I lift my eyes to the crucifix and wonder if it is meant as a warning, not a message of hope.

What will Luca think when he sees me like this?

I broke my promise. Let the dark in again.

And the money—Devel knows how much I spent.

Panic blooms. I claw through my pockets.

'No, no. Fucking no.'

Months. Months it took to save that money. Cold, wet nights. Sifting through darkness. Hunger, exhaustion, shame. Disappointing my kin. Skipping meals. Losing sleep. All of it —stolen by those fucking gadje pigs.

I can't face Luca. Not like this. Not again.

I stumble on, barely feeling my feet beneath me. I stop at the edge of the dirt path that leads down to the camp. Our tent stands alone. No fire. No voices. No life.

A sigh escapes my lips—relief, maybe—before the truth sets in.

They're really gone.

Teeth clenched against the pain, I sink to my haunches and press my hands to my head.

'What have I done?'

Rudi presses against my leg, warm and silent.

The night presses in—empty, still, bitter with frost.

No warmth. No welcome.

Only silence.

And me.

Alone again.

# CHAPTER SIX

*Broken and Bruised*

Sleep comes in shards, each one tipped with thoughts of Maria, Luca and the dead gadjo. Every sound—every shifting branch, every falling leaf—drags me out of slumber, breath held tight in hope or fear.

And each time, it's heartache. Just darkness and silence.

Long before dawn, I crawl out of the tent, jaw aching, head pounding. The bruising has my eyes nearly swollen shut, and my ribs grind with every stretch, every movement.

As a crimson crack splits the eastern sky, I start up the track with a bag on my back, Aisha's cane in hand, and Rudi at my heel. A hatchet tucked into my belt gives me some comfort. In my pocket, a coin—probably spilled from my moneybag last night—might be enough to buy something to dull the pain, maybe even something to sustain me through the morning.

Progress is slow. Each step brings a blinding rush of agony. Soon, my cheeks are streaked with tears, every movement punctuated by a grunt or moan. I glance skyward, searching for—I don't know what—but all I see are clouds swirling in all directions. A thick, grey soup stirred by some invisible force. No sign now of that promised morning sun.

'They broke something inside me,' I groan, glancing down at the limping dog. Rudi looks up with soft, wet eyes—suffering in silence, unlike me.

By the time I limp into town, I can see little beyond my own anguish. Light flashes at the corners of my eyes, pulsing and relentless. But I can hear the traders setting out their stalls, banging and clattering as they lay their stock out for the morning.

I stumble along, desperate to find anybody who might know something, but each time I look up at a trader, they turn away.

Then a lad comes trudging towards me with his head bent low and a sack over his shoulder. I stop him with a hand raised to his chest, but before I can speak, he spits at my feet and barges past. Fury flashes through my ribs like fire, and I yank him back by the scruff of his neck. The sack falls as he's jerked backwards.

'Little prick.' I tighten my grip, pressing my fingers into the soft flesh of his collar as Rudi lets out a low, loyal growl.

'Sorry,' the lad moans, and I raise a fist. That's when a hand lands on my shoulder, heavy and solid. I turn to see the butcher towering over me.

'Calm down,' the butcher says, lifting his hand from my shoulder and raising it to show he's not here for a fight. 'He's just a lad.'

I shake the boy a little—he's trembling now, eyes wide and wet—and release him, turning my attention to the big man before me, praying that he might know something.

'Look at the state of ye,' he says, turning then to see the lad on his way. 'Come with me.'

I follow the butcher, Rudi limping close behind.

The butcher leads me into the back of the stall and offers me a wooden chair.

'Your people, they left you behind.' He glances at me as he hefts a thick slab of meat onto a board. 'Am I right?'

I nod, the pain muting any expression.

'I seen them passing through here before sunup yesterday, heading west.' He raises a cleaver and brings it down on the meat with a clunk. 'I'm always the first here. I see everything that goes on.'

'Why are you helping me?'

He straightens, brushes splinters and dust from his hands, then reaches into a bucket. He pulls out a fist-sized bone—a joint of some sort, scraps of flesh still clinging to it—and tosses it to Rudi. Then he looks me in the eye.

'Your friend down the way, the dark-skinned gypsy—brought me soup when I was ill. Didn't even know my name. That's worth something.'

'She's not a gypsy,' I mumble, eyes on the dog.

He nods and shoves another log into the furnace. 'She's not from here either way.'

'Which way?' I ask.

'I told ye, *west*.' He scratches his head, then reaches down to scratch Rudi's. 'Best watch yourself. The authorities are after your kind.'

I stand, ready to go, but pause.

'Why?' I ask, immediately regretting the stupidity of the question. 'I mean, I know why. But what for?'

The butcher shrugs. 'All I know is what I've heard—they're taking kids and sending them away.'

I feel myself come apart at the seams, and the chair catches what's left of me. *New families?*

I set out with the butcher's warning ringing in my ears, the threads of my heart unravelling. Could it be that the gadje stole my family away? The thought chills me to the core.

No. I must believe that they are with Mama. And strangely, I find myself hoping that she was right all along. That she has taken them to keep them safe.

I arrive at Aisha's stall, but it looks empty. Lifting the cane, I run a hand along the carvings and lift the canvass to slip inside.

Rudi comes with me as lean in and prop the cane against a crate. He sniffs at the air and bristles, backing away. A low growl rumbles from his throat.

'What is it?' I whisper.

There's something strange in the air—a smell like iron, or incense, or both. I leave the cane and don't look back.

On the fringes of the market, I spot a shoddy stall selling home-brewed wine and ale. Long-necked bottles filled with cloudy red and brown. I stand and watch for a moment, overcome with a heavy numbness. I shouldn't. I know I shouldn't.

'Just to take the edge off,' I tell myself, limping forward.

As I approach, the man behind it eyes me with suspicion.

'My money's as good as any,' I say, cutting him off before

he can turn me away. I grab a bottle of wine by the neck and hand over my coin.

He lifts it to the dull daylight, bites down on the edge, then drops it into a tin and hands me my change.

I pull the cork out with my teeth and take a small sip. My head throbs the instant it touches my tongue—but it's too late now.

'Got any food?' I peer past him, scouring the back of the stall.

'Onion bread,' he grunts. 'Wife made it.'

I nod and hand back the change. He turns, takes a loaf from a linen bag and cuts a wedge off. Wrapped in greasy paper, he hands it to me, still warm.

The smell makes my stomach twist with hunger.

I unwrap it, take a bite, and wash it down with another sip of wine.

Then I'm back on the road—chewing, drinking, stumbling onward.

West takes me limping through fields and woodland, following the curve of a slow-paced river. Soon enough, I find cart tracks and hoofprints pressed into the dirt.

I finish the bread, down the wine, and toss the empty bottle into the water.

My pace quickens.

Pain fades.

Replaced by embers of hope.

And hot, bubbling rage.

The dull day slides into murky evening by the time I stumble upon the campsite. I'm greeted by the smell of smoke —stewed meat, damp wood burning. And there's music.

Fucking music.

I descend a small hill into the camp, losing my footing once or twice. Then I hobble between tents, Rudi still trailing behind, until I reach the fire.

Mama's easy to spot, sitting beside the fire, as always. Drinking her tea.

'Where are they?' I hiss.

She turns, her face a picture of surprise. 'Nura?'

She stands and comes to me, arms outstretched, a smile on her face—but I back away.

'We thought you left.' Then she sees my bruises and her smile falters. 'What happened?'

'Where's Maria?'

She scans my face. My broken lips. My blackened eyes, seeming not to hear the question.

I can't hold myself together any longer. I grab her shoulders and shake—like I'm trying to wake her from a dream.

'Mama, where are Luca and Maria?'

'They're not with you?' She brushes her thumbs beneath my eyes, like she could rub the bruises away. 'They stayed. Waited for you.'

'No more lies, Mama. You've been lying to me my whole life.'

She pulls away, but her eyes don't leave mine.

'You're just like your father.'

'Because I won't be fooled by you?'

'No.' Her voice hardens. 'Because you know less about this world than I've forgotten. Because you're ashamed to be Romani. And because you are blind to all you don't wish to see.'

'Dati was a good man,' I whisper, wiping tears from my cheeks. 'Don't talk about him that way.'

Mama fixes her gaze on me. There's venom in her eyes.

'Your father was a worthless drunk. And I smell the wine on your breath. You want to be a worthless drunk, too?'

'You abandoned them,' I snap. Grief and sorrow crashing against my anger.

My hand hangs by my side, and Rudi licks it.

I push him away, raise my hand, and slap Mama.

Just once.

She recoils, holding a hand to her cheek.

'You abandoned them to go hunting, remember?'

She comes forward, dropping her hand. 'We warned you that the gadje are coming,' she hisses, glancing back at Vaida. 'And now—Devel help you—you've lost the only thing that mattered.'

And I see now that Mama is crying.

I sink to my knees, pulled down by the weight in my chest, and pray this isn't true, as she slinks away.


My head spins at the thought of Maria being taken away, and I sink lower until I'm on my stomach, face pressed to the earth.

I feel sick. We've all heard the stories—Romani children snatched in the night, sent off to live on far-away farms. Parents dragged to the workhouses. Torn apart.

'No,' I breathe, shaking my head. 'No fucking way.'

I push up to my knees and look for Mama, but she is gone.

The other elders stare at me like I'm a stranger in their camp.

I clamber up and storm over to Mama's chipped and faded vardo. Red paint clings to the wood in desperate flakes —most of it stripped away by time. Time without Dati's care.

I take the steps and rip the door open. 'Where are they?'

Mama sits with a handkerchief pressed to her nose, and when I see her looking so feeble, all the fight is taken out of me.

'How could you leave them when you knew the dangers?'

Mama looks up at me, almost amused. 'Are you asking me, or yourself?'

I sink to my knees before her and clasp her hand in mine. 'Mama, they are all that matters in this world, and now they're gone.'

'My heart is broken, Nura.' She lets out a sob that feels like it's been suppressed for an age. 'I have a duty to the whole *kumpania — our community*. I can't endanger everyone else for the sake of two stubborn people. Even if they are your family.'

'Fuck, Mama, they're your family too.'

Whatever else she says is lost to the hiss that floods my head. I stumble outside and vomit — bile and wine and rage — and Rudi barks at the noise. My legs buckle and I collapse, crushed by the pain in my ribs, the throbbing in my skull, the fire in my leg.

Vaida lifts me from the dirt. My face slick with tears and spittle. All I want is to fold into myself, to close my eyes and sink into the earth.

I feel Mama's judgement radiating like smoke.

Drunken little bitch. Just like her father. No Romanipen.

I pull the hatchet from my waist, whistle for Rudi, and spit at the ground. 'I'll find them, Mama. But you'll never see us again.'

She just smirks, flashing the gaps in her teeth. 'Where would you even start, child? The bottom of a bottle?'

'I haven't had a drink in three years.'

'Until now.'

'Yes. Until now.'

Rudi returns to my side, and I limp away from the firelight and back towards town—back towards nothing.

I have no plan. No trail. No clue.

They could already be separated. Torn apart. Lost.

Rain comes cold and sharp as I hobble up the hill, the campsite shrinking behind me. It stings my hands and face— but the fire inside me burns hotter, driving me towards nowhere and everywhere at once. Every moment without Maria is a stitch in my heart, pulling tighter with each step.

I walk until the tavern looms before me. My heart hammers against my ribs. With rain-numbed fingers, I touch the hardwood handle of my hatchet and glance down at Rudi.

'You ready?' I ask, masking the tremor in my voice.

He cocks his head. Loyal. Confused. Ready.

I push through the door.

The stairwell reeks—sour ale, piss, something worse. My throat tightens, the stink flaring the bruises on my face. I touch my jaw. Swollen. Tender. Forgotten pain remembered all at once. Rudi's ears are pricked. He senses what I do. Hostility.

I peel back my wet hood, open the second door, and stride in like I've nothing to lose.

The first face I see is the innkeeper's. He stumbles around the bar, both hands raised.

'Whoa there. No more trouble,' he says, backing up. 'If you've got a gang of gypsies up there, keep 'em up there.'

Behind him, the room stirs. Shifty glances. Hands

tightening around mugs.

'I've nobody with me.'

'Then you definitely need to leave.'

I shove him aside and limp to the bar. 'Two nights back —maybe the early hours of yesterday—the authorities came for my family.' I sweep the room with a hard stare. 'I need to know where they've been taken.'

A voice snaps from the back: 'Fuck off.'

'Gypsy scum. I hope they hang.'

Blood rushes to my ears. The pain returns—sharp, hot, blinding. And then a hand grabs my shoulder, yanks me backwards.

I throw an elbow, hard. It cracks against the innkeeper's face. He stumbles, and in one smooth motion, I draw my hatchet and bring it down—clean—on his hand.

Flesh splits. Blood follows.

He hits the ground screaming, clutching the split hand. I step over him, Rudi snarling at my heel.

'I don't have time to play,' I snarl. 'Tell me what I need to know. Or I'll hack this prick into pieces.'

'Fuck off bitch, we don't know anything.'

'No?' I turn to the cowering innkeeper and drive my fist into his gaunt face. His nose crunches beneath the weight of my hatchet-clutching hand.

A gasp cuts through the room. The innkeeper lets out a strangled moan as he rocks backwards.

'Still nothing?' I stomp on his crotch, then his knee. He howls for help, and the room shifts—men rising reluctantly from their stools—but Rudi growls low, his warning clear.

I raise the hatchet. 'I'll ask one more time. Then he loses a limb.'

The man curls inward, tucking his hands under his belly,

whimpering.

'They're gone.'

The voice comes from the shadows. A man steps into the flickering light—and I recognise him as a market trader.

'They came through before dawn,' he says. 'Wagon full of gypsies surrounded by magistrate's men. Priest was with them. He seemed to be the one in charge.'

'Where did they go?'

The trader glances down at the wrecked innkeeper and shakes his head. 'You shouldn't have done this.'

'They took my daughter.' I advance, hatchet rising again. 'Where. Did. They. Take. Her?'

'I don't know. Nobody knows.' He brushes past me and squats by the innkeeper.

'The priest—did you recognise him?'

'I seen him in church,' the man mutters. 'The big one in the square.'

Behind me, Rudi barks. Sharp. Warning.

I spin and see them—at least five men creeping closer, one of them the brute from last night.

I lurch forward, thrusting the hatchet up to his throat. He stumbles back. Tries to swing. I catch his wrist, deflect the blow, and grab his collar.

'You've got something of mine,' I growl, dragging him closer to the blade.

He fumbles in his pockets, then hands over my rings, his eyes darting to the door behind me.

'I was gonna give it back,' he whines.

I cock my head. Let the silence hang.

'And my coin?'

He digs in another pocket and pulls out a few coppers. 'It's all I've got left.'

I snatch them from his hand and back up to the door, dragging him with me. Rudi plants himself between me and the others, a growl rumbling like thunder in his chest.

I shove the man to his knees, whistle for Rudi, and spin towards the exit —

And there's Aisha, holding the door open.

She yanks me through, flashes a smile, and slams it behind us — wedging my hatchet through the handle so clean and fast I don't even register her taking it.

We sprint up the stairs and out onto the rain-soaked street.

It won't take them long to break through the door.

We need to run.

I turn to Aisha — so many questions rising in my throat — but she just pulls up her hood and grabs my arm, dragging me into the nearest alley.

Then another.

And another after that.

We snake through the town like shadows. My chest thunders with the beat of my heart. Sweat burns my face despite the drizzling rain. A glance down shows blood spattered across my midriff — dark, drying, not mine.

It takes a dozen more turns before I'm calm enough to breathe.

I slip my rings back onto my fingers and give Rudi a scratch behind the ear.

'Have you been following me?'

Aisha studies me for a long beat, her eyes sharp and unreadable. 'You're fiercer than you look, Nura.'

'That's not an answer.'

'Let's just say, I have a nose for trouble.'

It's all she gives me.

I open my palm, weigh the few coppers she helped me salvage. Nothing close to what I had—but enough, maybe, to keep me upright for another day.

Maria. Luca. The fucking priest.

The alley opens up onto the main square, wide and wet, lit by oil lamps that flicker like watchful eyes. I emerge in a far corner of the town square, opposite the church, my leg screaming at me to rest.

Between me and it stands a modest fountain, its slick stone glinting in the light.

'I'd stay away from the church tonight,' Aisha says quietly.

I ignore her. Step forward. Rudi follows.

Then I see it—just to the side of the entrance. A structure, tall and wooden, silhouetted against the stone. And something hangs from it.

Spindling in the breeze.

My breath catches in my throat.

I freeze. Can't move forward. Can't look away. My heart clenches into a fist.

Too tall to be Maria.

Too small to be Luca.

I drift closer. Not to the church now, but the gallows.

The woman hanging there turns slightly in the wind.

And I collapse. Not to the ground, but inside myself. Tears stream down my cheeks before I even feel them.

'They found her guilty of being a witch,' comes a voice beside me.

I flinch—Aisha, again, appearing like a ghost.

'She wasn't, of course. But she represented something they didn't understand.' She takes my hand in hers, gentle and firm. 'These are dangerous times.'

I wipe my face with a shaking hand. My lips part before I can stop them.

I tell her about Maria. About Luca. About the priest. About my plan to storm the church.

'You'll end up like her if you try,' Aisha says, nodding to the gallows. She gives my arm a gentle tug, drawing me back from the brink.

'But I can help you find them.'

# CHAPTER SEVEN

## *The Order of the Kresnik*

'You know where they were taken?'

Her golden clothes shimmer in the dark as she takes my hand and gives a gentle tug.

'We need to go.'

Male voices echo through the alleys behind us—angry, searching. She pulls me into a narrow passage between stone buildings, down a flight of cracked concrete steps, and onto a track that stretches into the farmland beyond.

'Where are you taking me?' I ask, the protest half-hearted. 'I need to find my family.'

'You will,' she says. 'But not alone. Not like this.'

We cross a humped bridge swallowed in shadow, the wood creaking beneath us. On the far side, she veers into a field where tall grass parts into a faint trail. Rudi darts ahead, chasing unseen shapes in the wheat.

A sweet, sour scent hits me as we step into a summer orchard. Overripe apples rot beneath the trees, and something bolts from the shadows. I reach for my hatchet just as Rudi takes off after it.

'A deer,' Aisha whispers. 'Feeding on the apples.'

My heart slows. I glance at the ground—apples everywhere, hundreds of them softening in the dirt. A path has been trampled through them, though a few roll loose beneath our steps.

'Is this your orchard?'

'In a sense.'

'Why don't you gather the fruit?'

'We are not farmers.'

'Everybody knows how to pick apples.'

'We harvest something else.'

That gives me pause. I let it hang between us as we walk. Each step bruises the fruit underfoot. Aisha moves like water —steady, silent. I stumble more than once.

We emerge from the last row of trees onto a gravel path that crunches beneath our boots. Ahead, a stone farmhouse rises from the gloom.

'Are you going to tell me what you know now?'

'Inside,' she says, and takes my hand again.

She unlocks the door and leads me into the darkness.

'This is your house?'

'For now.'

She moves through the shadows like she owns them, lighting candles with practised grace. The flickering light reveals a small hearth, a battered table with chairs, and a heavy wooden chest pressed against the wall.

Aisha slips off her cloak, folds it neatly, and places it atop the chest.

'Where's your dog?' she asks.

'He likes to keep guard.'

I hover near the fire, clenching and unclenching my fists.

'Tell me what you know.'

'In time.'

She takes two cups from a cubby, pours a dark liquid that could be wine, and offers one to me.

'You'll need it,' she says.

I set the cup on the chest, untouched. My fingers are still sticky with blood.

A flicker of the innkeeper's face rises unbidden—his sobs, the way he cowered. I shove it down.

'This is a waste of time.'

I turn for the door, hands trembling. 'I have to find my daughter.'

'They started taking children ten years ago, in India.'

Her words stop me cold, my hand on the doorframe.

'They've gotten good at it. You won't find her. Not without our help.'

I turn to face her.

'Our?'

'They moved through India like a plague,' Aisha says. 'Then across the rest of Asia and into Europe. Now they're here.'

'Who's here?' I turn back into the room, rage prickling just beneath my skin. It's all I can do not to seize her by the throat and shake the truth out.

'Vampyres,' a voice says behind me.

I spin. A hulking man fills the doorway, pale and broad-shouldered, with blonde hair hanging over one eye.

'Jakub,' Aisha says with a smile. 'Where's your sister?'

'Outside,' he replies, eyes on me, a smirk pulling at one

corner of his mouth.

'Playing with the puppy.' He steps inside, boots heavy on the floorboards.

'It's good to see you, Aisha.'

'Did you say vampyres?' I watch her closely, waiting for the punchline.

But she doesn't blink.

'This is bullshit,' I snap. 'Maria's out there—alone—and you bring me here to talk about monsters and myths?'

'This is no joke,' Aisha says.

Jakub pulls her into a bear-hug, kisses each of her cheeks. 'We've missed you.'

'I've been busy.'

He nods in my direction. 'Who's your jumpy friend?'

Aisha's gaze softens, those deep brown eyes brimming with sorrow. 'They took her daughter.'

'Vampyres?' I shoot back, my hand flying to my belt for a hatchet that isn't there.

'What the hell is going on?'

'First,' a voice says behind me, calm but firm, 'let us explain who we are.'

I turn again—another presence in the doorway. A man in a brown suit, tall and thin, steps into the candlelight. A lean blonde woman follows, quiet and sharp-eyed. Rudi pads in behind them, and suddenly I feel hemmed in on all sides.

'Please sit,' Aisha says, gesturing to the table.

Something in her voice stops me. Not force—something else. Gravity. I sit.

'Someone tell me how to get my daughter back,' I say. My voice shakes, but the edge beneath it is real.

The suited man drags a chair to the table and lowers himself into it. He removes his hat and places it carefully on the wood. A long scar cuts through one eye like lightning.

'You've heard of vampyres, yes? Revenants. Nosferatu.'

I glance at Aisha. 'Faeries and witches, too. Baba Yaga—that was always my favourite tale.'

'This is no tale,' Jakub growls.

Aisha lowers her gaze. 'We lost someone today.'

I know who she means.

'The woman in the square. She was one of us. The only soul in this godforsaken town brave enough to help.' She swallows. 'They tortured her. Took her eyes. God knows what else—before they hanged her.'

My stomach turns. I see her again, spinning at the end of a rope.

'Would she have revealed anything about us?' the man in the suit asks.

'She didn't know anything about us,' Aisha says, sitting opposite me.

She reaches for my hand. Her skin is warm. Steady. 'I'm telling you this, so you understand how serious it is, Nura.'

I pull my hand away and glance down, making sure Rudi is still at my side.

'So vampyres took my family, that's what you're telling me?'

My voice is low, almost too quiet to hear. A beat of silence.

'Yes,' Aisha replies.

I stare at her. My fists clench in my lap.

'I came here for answers,' I mutter. 'Not bedtime stories.'

'It's true,' Aisha replies.

I shake my head, a dry laugh escaping. It cracks on its way out. 'No. No, this is madness.'

'Be on your way then,' Jakub growls. 'We have more

pressing concerns.'

'No.' Aisha's voice cuts through him like a blade. 'I gave her my word.'

I glance between them, chest rising and falling, fists clenched. 'Who are you people?'

'We are the Order of the Kresnik,' the suited man says, folding his hands over his knee. 'Or... what's left of the order.'

'Vampyre hunters,' Aisha cuts in. 'We've tracked this particular faction across continents. For decades.'

The man leans into the candlelight, and I notice the tattoos on his hands—an open skull, a blood-tipped sword.

'Truth is,' he continues, 'there aren't enough of us left. We're stretched thin, and they're everywhere.' His eyes linger on Aisha, warm despite the frost in his voice. 'She brought us together again. Across oceans. Across grief.'

'Unfortunate for you, then,' Jakub says, 'that you're caught in the middle of this war.'

'Unfortunate?' My voice sharpens into a snarl. 'They have my fucking child. You say you hunt monsters—so hunt them.'

Jakub chuckles, thumping a hand on the table. 'I like this one. She's fiery.'

The tall blonde woman—Jakub's sister, I guess—takes my hand and presses the cup of wine into it. Her touch is light but firm. She pours one for herself.

'I'm Alfie Robinson,' the suited man says. 'You've met Jakub. This is Renata, his twin.'

They nod—Jakub with a grin, Renata with barely a blink.

'Once,' Alfie says, 'I was principal among the Kresnik of the British Empire. Jakub and Renata covered Eastern

Europe. And Aisha...' He looks to her, reverently. 'The most feared Virangana in the subcontinent.'

'We had thousands in our ranks. Hunters across the globe. But evil is tireless. And this... this is not a profession that promotes longevity.' He takes a sip of wine, then reaches up, absent-minded, to trace the scar that splits his face.

'We are all that's left.'

Aisha turns back to me. 'What Alfie is trying to say is—there's no hope of finding your family without us.'

I down the wine in one gulp and pour another with shaking hands. 'The authorities took them. People saw it happen.'

Jakub leans forward, arms flexing against the edge of the table. 'You are naïve.'

'Jakub,' Aisha warns, placing a calm hand on his arm.

He rises and steps back, brooding. Renata takes his place at the table.

'With the help of my informant,' Aisha says, 'I've learned much about the Carmilla's operations here in Hungary, and beyond.' Her expression darkens. 'They've embedded themselves into government. Law enforcement. And the church.'

'The church?' Alfie murmurs, hand drifting to the silver cross around his neck.

'It gets worse,' Aisha says. 'They've used that influence to create a legal system. One that justifies taking Romani children. Not just here, but all across Europe.'

'Bastards,' Alfie growls, voice rough with restrained fury.

'Why?' I ask, almost afraid of the answer.

'Indoctrination,' Aisha says. 'They raise them far from any human influence. They're taught obedience. Loyalty.'

I shake my head. 'No. That's not —'

'It's what they do,' Alfie interrupts. 'It's how they've lasted. How they've multiplied. An army of conditioned monsters.'

'And the men?' I ask.

A silence falls. Jakub finally speaks.

'Thralls.'

Just one word. Cold and final.

We all look at him. Waiting. But he says nothing more.

Archie and Aisha lock eyes in a silence that stretches too long. I sit frozen, breath caught in my chest.

'How do I get my baby back?' my voice splinters.

Aisha leans forward, her voice soft but certain. 'The good news is — you have time. They like to raise the children. Let them grow… before —'

'Before what?' I snap. My voice cuts through the air like a whip. I glance around at the scarred, tired faces gathered in this flickering lamplight. A knot tightens in my stomach.

'What do they do to the children?'

Aisha looks away. Even Jakub's cocky grin has faded. Only Alfie meets my eyes.

'They're turned,' he says. 'Made into vampyres to swell the ranks. Once it happens… they remember nothing of who they were.'

I swallow the lump in my throat. Focus. She said I have time.

'And Luca?' I ask. 'What do they do with the men?'

'These aren't just monsters in storybooks,' Alfie says. 'They're real. And they're worse.'

'He's dead?' I whisper.

'Enthralled,' Renata answers coldly.

'What does that mean?'

Aisha reaches for my hand again. 'They cast a blood spell. It severs the mind. Turns them into slaves.'

'So he's alive?' I ask, barely breathing.

'There's no coming back from it.' Renata's voice is almost too quiet to hear. 'He's as good as dead.'

I turn, pointing a shaking finger at her. 'What did you just say?'

Before she can answer, Aisha grips my shoulder—not hard, but firm. Grounding. 'Stay. Rest. We'll find the truth together.'

Behind us, Jakub clomps around the kitchen like a bear. 'Got any food?'

'Bread and stew,' Aisha replies. 'Let me warm it.'

She moves to the hearth and strikes a flint. The fire crackles to life behind me—but I barely hear it. My thoughts spin around Luca.

'A slave?' I murmur. 'For what?'

'Whatever they need,' Alfie says. 'That's how they operate. They enthral the living. Use them to do their bidding. After that...' He sighs, voice low and grave. 'The best they can hope for is death.'

He reaches for my hand again. 'I'm sorry, my dear.'

I pull away.

'Fuck this.' I rise to my feet. My voice shakes with fury. 'Give me a weapon.'

'You don't understand,' Alfie says. 'Vampyres aren't myths. They're terrifying. Stronger than anything you've seen. You wouldn't last five seconds—'

'I'm not sitting here all night talking about it,' I snap. 'While they have my daughter.'

I whistle for Rudi and start for the door.

'You'll die out there.' Aisha lunges after me, grabs my

wrist. 'Just listen. Alfie's right. We've fought them for a very long time.'

'Then you know what I'm up against. And still you'd keep me here?' I yank my wrist free and throw open the door. Cold air slams into me like a slap. 'She's out there. And I have to go.'

Alfie steps up beside me, sliding his hat back on. 'Before you do—there's someone you need to meet. One more member of our little group.'

I pause. The cold bites deeper than the claws. 'Who?'

He glances out into the blackness. 'Someone the vampyres fear more than any of us.'

'Who?' I mutter, just as Rudi begins to growl into the dark.

'When a vampyre bites,' Alfie says, stepping out beside me, 'one of two things happens: the victim either dies or becomes a vampyre themselves.'

The air is ice cold. My fingers curl into my armpits as frost settles into my bones. My breath hangs, clouding the night.

'But on very rare occasions,' Alfie continues, 'something else happens. The victim doesn't die. Doesn't turn. Not quite.' He scans the treeline. 'A creature of the night, yes. But human enough to resist the hunger.'

Then, out of nowhere, something shifts on the path ahead. A figure appears—hooded and still. My stomach lurches. I stumble back.

Alfie catches me, his fingers hot on my arms.

'These rare beings have all the physical strength of a vampyre,' he murmurs, 'but something inside them clings to the human soul.'

The figure moves—gliding, not walking. Graceful.

Controlled. Predatory.

'You could count them on one hand,' Alfie says, smirking slightly. I glance down.

Rudi is calm, watching the creature from beside me. I've never seen him so still.

'What the hell is that?' I whisper.

'She has power over the living.'

Alfie lets go of me.

And then I feel it—something in my head. Slithering. Coiling. My thoughts grind against pressure that's not mine. I clutch my temples and force myself not to scream. Not to run.

I stand. And fight it.

The figure stops a stone's throw away, shrouded in mist like a statue chiselled from shadow.

'So, what—she's a good vampyre?'

Alfie laughs softly, then grips my wrist and tugs me forward.

'She lost her whole family to the Carmillas,' he says. 'I believe it was rage—pure, relentless rage—that kept her soul from being consumed.'

Each step I take makes my blood feel colder. My teeth chatter. My hands tremble.

The creature lifts its head. Pale as spider eggs, her eyes lock on mine.

She has a small nose, a narrow mouth. White hair spills from her hood in soft waves. Her skin looks drained of life— porcelain turned to ash.

'Nura,' Alfie says, 'this is Lina. The dhampir. Vengeance manifest.'

Terror claws at my skin, rattles my bones, but I can't look away.

There's nothing on her face. No kindness. No cruelty. Just purpose.

'She hunts vampyres?' I ask, my voice dry as bone.

'We hunt the day. She stalks the night.'

A silence stretches. Her eyes never leave mine. A mirror. A warning.

I blink. Step back. Something in my chest twists tight.

I tear my gaze away and turn my back. 'As long as she doesn't get in my way.'

I stride back to the cottage. Rudi snaps out of his trance and follows. The frost bites at my back, but I barely feel it.

Aisha waits in the doorway, eyes wide, studying me.

'How did you do that?' she asks.

'I need a weapon.' I shoulder past, grab the wine from the table, and drink.

Aisha crosses to a panel in the rear wall. She opens a hidden door and retrieves a blade—a strange sword with curved blade and yellow grip.

'Ever seen one of these?' she asks.

I shake my head. The others gather close.

'It's an Indian talwar,' she says, brushing her fingers along the blade. An inscription glows faintly in the lamplight. 'Inlaid with silver. More lethal than any ordinary steel.'

Alfie bursts through the door behind us, face pale, shivering hard. 'How did you do that?' he asks.

'Do what?' I don't even look at him.

'She compelled you to stay. And you walked away.'

Aisha hands me the sword. I lift it, test the weight, feel the balance. The blade is chipped. A little rust lines the edge. But it feels right in my hand.

Like it's meant to be there.

'Dunno,' I mutter. 'Didn't feel compelled to stay.'

'Are you mad?' Jakub steps into my path. 'You're giving her weapons?'

'She fights the same fight we do,' Aisha replies. 'And you just saw for yourselves—she's strong.'

'She'll die before she gets to swing that thing.' He reaches for the sword.

I twist away, holding the blade close. 'Don't make me try this thing.'

Jakub backs away.

'Where is she even going?' he growls.

'I'm going to kill the bastards that took my family,' I snap. 'And if you don't step aside, I'll start with you.'

Jakub takes a breath, draws himself up, and steps forward.

'Stop!' Alfie roars.

The room falls still.

Breathing hard, I drop my glare from Jakub's eyes, as Aisha presses something into my hand—a worn leather scabbard. I fasten it around my waist, tucking the blade into place as I stride for the door. Rudi trails behind me, a deep growl humming in his chest.

'Wait,' Aisha calls. 'Take a horse from the stable.'

'A fucking horse now too?' Jakub barks, storming into the kitchen and kicking a chair across the floor.

Aisha doesn't flinch. Her voice drops. 'We have an extra.'

I hesitate at the doorway.

'Where?'

'Round back. There's a path to the stable. Take the black Hucul.' She meets my eyes. 'I have a feeling you two will get along.'

# CHAPTER EIGHT

*Ghosts of the Stable*

As I approach the stable, the stink of horse shit makes me smile. It reminds me of my childhood—when we had horses of our own to tend, and Dati would take me riding. Long summer days on horseback, talking and laughing. Me up front, him behind. Through pastures and orchards, eating whatever we could reach.

I remember the smell of sun-warmed stone as we sat overlooking the valley. The warmth of his hands. The way his flask glinted in the light. The way it bobbed in the water the day he died.

His lifeless body face-down in a shallow stream, the same one we'd splashed in as children.

The great man who taught me everything—undone by drink and a river no deeper than my knees.

Rudi's bark pulls me back. My breath rasps in my throat.

The horses fret behind the stable wall. I stand there, fingers curled around the hilt, head pounding. And then the grief comes—flooding, raw. I punch the stable wall. Again. And again.

Knuckles crack. Splinters bite. I scream until my voice gives out.

When I can't lift my arms anymore, I drop to the straw-covered ground in a broken heap.

I can't lose anyone else. Especially not Maria.

So I rise. Bloodied. Breathless. And I turn to the horses.

Rain begins to fall, cold and needle-sharp, as I lead the black Hucul from the last stall. He nickers and pulls against the lead, but I calm him with a firm hand and saddle him using the old leather tack hanging on the rail. It creaks, but it holds. He lets me climb up.

Hood up. Head down. I ride into the night.

The talwar at my side is awkward, heavy, but I welcome the discomfort. The horse is bigger than the one I rode as a girl, less forgiving—but part of me wishes it were daytime, just so I could ride straight through the market square.

Let them see me now.

Soon I'm back in the town square, staring up at the hanged woman. Aisha was right—her face has been mutilated.

I dismount and move closer.

Her hands are tied behind her back. Several fingers are missing. Dried blood crusts at the corners of her mouth.

Tears roll down my cheeks as I lift my gaze to the looming church doors. My hands tremble.

Soon, a thin streak of sunlight splits the gloom. The church towers over me, its oak doors massive and arched, split in two down the centre.

I tie the horse to a hitching post and pull one of the heavy doors open. It groans against the frame.

I step inside, leaving Rudi at the threshold.

A rush of air disturbs the lamps and candles within. They flicker wildly.

The air is thick—warm, musty. Wings beat somewhere high in the rafters.

I take a moment to scan the walls. Painted saints. Cosmas and Damian. Others I don't know. The work is fine, reverent.

Then a voice cuts through the stillness.

'The Lord never sleeps,' it says.

I turn. A man in white priest's robes stands behind me. Dark eyes. Black hair peppered with grey, falling past his cheeks.

'But priests do,' he adds, smiling. 'Luckily for you, I never miss a sunrise.'

'Lucky,' I reply, stalking forwards. My fingers tightening into fists.

He steps closer, arms out, palms turned up—like he means to receive me. Or bless me. Or disarm me.

'An early morning confession is good for the soul,' he says. 'Young sinner, take a knee.'

I stop just short of him.

'But I'm not here to confess,' I whisper.

'I'm here to hear yours, Father.'

His smile vanishes. His eyes flick to the blade at my waist. He takes a step back.

'What madness is this?' the priest stammers.

I lunge.

Fingers close around his robe. I yank him forwards and drive my elbow into his eye socket. His knees buckle. Only my grip keeps him from collapsing.

'Tell me what you know.'

I punch him in the chest. He crumples.

'Tell me!'

He squirms in my hands, trying to crawl backwards. 'Please—take what you want. The collection box—it's yours.'

'I'm not here for your fucking money,' I snarl. 'What do you know about the woman outside?'

He simpers through a bloodied mouth. 'She was a witch. And a whore.'

I kick him hard between the legs and let him fall.

He rolls onto his back, wheezing. 'Not by me. I didn't lay a hand on her.'

'But you didn't stop it.'

He crawls towards the altar. Whimpering. I follow.

My fingers wrap around the hilt of the talwar as I slide it from its sheath.

Steel sings in the candlelight.

He drags himself to the first step and turns back to me.

'Please,' he gasps.

Morning light spills through the stained-glass, casting crimson across his face.

'Where did they take the children?'

'I don't know anything about any children.' His hands rise—pathetic, trembling.

'You've made a mistake, please—'

I drive my fist into his face. His skull thuds against the altar. He groans, sagging sideways.

'They have my husband and daughter.'

He wipes at his bleeding nose, snarling, 'This is a house of God! Damn you for spilling blood here—'

I raise the blade to his throat.

He falls silent.

For a heartbeat, I hover there—steel against skin, lies hanging between us.

He looks up at me, eyes wet and wide. And still, somewhere inside me, I want to feel sorry for him.

But I can't.

Not after what he allowed. Not with what he knows.

He sees it in my eyes.

'There's nothing—'

I pull the blade back.

Slash.

A blur of silver and a spray of red.

He screams, clutching his hand as fingers hit the floor. The colour drains from his face.

'My—f...fingers...' he whimpers.

'Tell me what you know.' I raise the blade again. 'Or your head will be next.'

'I had no choice!' He collapses sideways, sobbing. 'Please. I didn't want this.'

I step closer. The tip of the sword hovers inches from his throat.

'Start talking. Everything.'

'It was the bishop. He gave the order. More children. Gypsy children.'

Something hollow opens inside me. A pit.

'Why?'

'I don't know,' he whines, waving his mangled hands in front of his face. 'We used to send them to proper homes. For assimilation. But now... now they're sent to a monastery.'

'What monastery? Where?'

'I don't know the name. It doesn't have one!'

He's trembling, snot and blood running down his chin. 'I

was there once. It's a day or two north by horseback.'

'Nearest town?'

He stares at the rafters as if salvation lives up there.

'Gyor,' he breathes.

'And your part in this?'

'Nothing. I signed things. Papers. I looked away. That's all, I swear.'

'You call that nothing?' My voice is a growl now.

He tries to rise to his knees. 'They're better off—those children. They'd have died in the gutters or been lost to sin.'

He's not entirely wrong. I wanted to leave myself.

But this is my family we're talking about.

'And what of the woman outside?' I cock my head, raise the talwar to his throat again. 'Is she better off?'

'Her fate was sealed by the courts,' he mutters. 'Guilty of witchcraft. And whoring.'

'Is that right?'

My jaw aches from clenching. There's a dull throb behind my eyes.

I press the blade to his belly. Hard.

'Let's hope the Lord looks more kindly on your deeds, Father.'

'No—' comes a voice behind me.

I spin.

Aisha stands in the aisle, hood up, robes of ember and blood flowing around her.

'What are you doing here?'

'If you kill him,' she says, stepping closer, 'the church will never stop hunting you. You'll die before you see your daughter again.'

She's calm, but I can hear it—that tiny thread of fear in her voice. For me.

'He's told you what he knows,' she says. 'Don't put yourself at risk now.'

'What he knows is enough to hang him twice.'

'We can only fight one war at a time.' She places a hand on my shoulder, trying to anchor me. 'First the Carmillas. Then the church.'

'The church is the enemy,' I hiss. 'Didn't you hear him? He confessed. They took my family.'

I tighten my grip on the talwar.

His eyes are pleading now. Hands shaking. Blood on his lips.

Somewhere deep inside me, a voice whispers, *don't do it.*

I don't know if it's Dati's voice. Or Mama's. Or Maria's.

I hold the blade steady. My hand trembles.

He signed the papers.

I grit my teeth.

He turned his face, pretended not to see.

One deep breath.

Then I drive the blade forward.

The priest's breath bursts out in a wet gasp as the talwar slices through his gut. He clutches at the wound, blood spilling between his fingers like dark silk.

He slumps back against the altar, mouth moving in a prayer he doesn't finish.

I wipe the blade on his robe.

'What have you done?' Aisha kneels beside him, eyes wide. 'We don't just murder people.'

I smirk. Cold. Detached.

'Don't you hunt monsters?' I point at the dying priest as she glares up at me. 'That's one less.'

'This isn't justice,' she says quietly, hands stained red. 'You've started a war we can't win.'

I turn away, hiding the shake in my legs, and grab the wooden collection box on my way to the door.

'What now?' Aisha hisses.

I smash the box on the stone floor. Coins scatter.

'They used it for evil,' I say, scooping the money into my purse. 'We'll use it for war.'

Outside, I mount the black Hucul just as Aisha steps out of the church—blood-smeared and furious. She opens her mouth, no doubt ready to lecture me on who I can and can't kill, but I don't give her the chance.

'Thanks for your help, and goodbye.'

'I'm coming with you,' she says, swinging up onto her chestnut mare.

'I've no use for faerie tales or witch hunts.' I press a heel to the horse and start north, gripping the reins tight to steady my shaking hands. 'I appreciate the help, but I'm going to find my family. And I don't think you've got the stomach for what that'll take.'

Aisha rides up beside me, laughing quietly as she wipes her bloodied hands on a rag from her saddlebag—one, then the other. 'You've no idea what I've got the stomach for. And even less idea what's waiting for you at that monastery.'

'You're right. I don't know you. And you don't know me.'

I glance at her, the words hard and final. 'Come if you want—but understand this. I'll do whatever it takes to get them back. Whatever it takes.'

Aisha nods once, pulling her shawl up over her head as the wind picks up.

'Then we'd best put some distance between us and what's left of that priest.'

\* \* \*

We ride side by side in silence until the sun sits high in the sky and my stomach aches with hunger. The Hucul grows irritable, tossing his head, tugging at the reins, veering off path. Finally, we reach a small hamlet—a smudge on the road, barely more than a dozen houses—but it has a tavern, and that's enough for me.

You can see the whole place from horseback. There's a trough, a hitching post on either side of it.

We dismount, tie the horses, and let Rudi drink—but I keep one hand on the talwar's grip as we cross the threshold.

'Pull your hood up,' Aisha mutters, already scanning the windows. I obey.

The smell of stewed meat hits me like a punch. My stomach growls, but I don't let myself relax.

Behind the counter, a plump barmaid offers a forced smile. Her eyes linger too long on my sword.

I scan the room—a handful of patrons, none armed. One near the fire with twitchy hands. Two by the bar, whispering. The others don't look up.

We take the farthest table. My back to the wall. I place the weapon beside me, close.

I don't sit fully. More like I perch. Eyes still on the door.

The barmaid approaches, her face shiny with sweat. 'Ale or wine?'

'Water,' Aisha replies.

'Ale,' I add, ignoring the glare Aisha shoots me.

The woman leans in, conspiratorial. 'You'll find no trouble in here.' She gestures for us to lower our hoods. 'Be comfortable.'

I glance around, then nod and pull mine back. Aisha follows, unwrapping her shawl.

'Is the stew good?'

'Best in the province.'

'I'll take a bowl.' I slide a coin across the table and look to Aisha. She shakes her head.

'None for me.' She offers the barmaid a polite smile, then pulls a drawstring bag from her satchel.

'You don't like stew?'

'Where I'm from, many people live and die without ever tasting meat.' She pours a handful of nuts into her palm. 'I choose not to, out of respect for them.'

I snort. 'Where I'm from, you eat what's put in front of you.'

The stew arrives, thick and steaming, with a wedge of bread and a battered spoon. The barmaid returns with the beer. I feel Aisha watching me, but I drink deep anyway and dig in.

As I eat, all I can think of is Maria. Of the meals we shared. Her laughter. Her little hands reaching for warm bread. Each bite twists something deeper in my chest. The thread pulls tighter. Harder.

I drop the spoon and down the ale in one long gulp.

'We'll find them,' Aisha says gently.

Her hand rests on mine, tattooed fingers curling around my wrist. A demon stares up at me in ink.

'Do you really believe all this? The vampyres, the dhampir?'

'You saw her with your own eyes. Felt her inside your head.'

'I saw something,' I admit. 'Doesn't make it true.'

Aisha smiles, calm and knowing. 'You'll know soon enough.'

I glance at the talwar. 'Whoever's holding my family, *they* will know soon enough. *They* will feel my fury.'

'And they should be afraid,' Aisha says, sipping her water. 'You have a gift.'

I snort, wiping my mouth. 'You're starting to sound like my dati.'

'Maybe he saw what you're still trying to ignore.'

I push the bowl aside. 'I'm not joining your crusade, Aisha. I don't have time to believe in anything but getting my family back.'

'I was like you once,' she says, reaching again. 'Lost. Alone. Stubborn.'

I stand, cutting her off. Gather my weapon and the bread. My voice low.

'I'm not stubborn. I'm running out of time.'

We return to the horses. I stash the bread in my saddlebag and ride on.

'Reckless, then,' Aisha says, raising my chagrin.

'What you did to that priest, it will have consequences.'

'What he did had consequences,' I clap back.

The road narrows as we leave the hamlet, winding through farmland towards the horizon. Fields on either side. Forest beyond. Mountains to the west.

We ride in silence. Me ahead, Aisha close behind. The sun blazes overhead as the road sinks down into a valley.

Aisha's words echo, needling me. *Stubborn.*

It's not the first time I've heard it. But what other choice do I have? I can't stop. Not now.

Then Rudi veers suddenly off the track, nose to the wind, ears pricked. He bolts into the tall grass.

Aisha catches up just as the sound reaches us— thundering hooves, men shouting.

Two riders barrel down the hill behind us, Arabian mounts foaming at the bit. Behind them, a wagon crests the ridge.

'Churchmen,' I gasp.

'Go,' Aisha mutters. Her eyes meet mine. 'Go now.'

I kick the Hucul into motion, and it eats up the road ahead until we're in the deepest pit of the valley and face the long climb up.

One rider halts mid-slope. A shot cracks the sky. The other charges after us.

I urge the horse harder, but the Hucul's fighting the incline. We won't outrun them.

'The forest,' Aisha shouts.

I pull the reins hard and swerve into the field, grass parting like water. Rudi streaks ahead, barking.

Behind me, I hear them closing the gap. The wagon creaks to a halt on the road.

'Stop! Murderer!' a voice roars. 'Face your judgement!'

Another shot cracks the air. The lead zips past my ear. I nearly lose my seat and swing to the right.

The Hucul's foaming now, breath heaving, legs shaking— but we burst through the trees into the woods.

We're not safe. Not yet.

I draw the talwar, pat the horse's neck. 'Sorry, boy.'

I nick his flank with the blade. He bolts forwards, nearly unseating me.

'Gypsy!' someone yells behind us. 'You'll hang for what you've done!'

I risk a glance back and see Aisha isn't fleeing. She stopped on the road, bow in hand.

She draws an arrow tipped with something strange— flute-shaped, with black twine trailing like a fuse.

She lets the arrow fly. It arcs through the air—lands short.

Then—

The road erupts.

Flame and thunder. My horse rears, screaming. I nearly bite my tongue in two. Almost topple from the horse as it bolts into the trees.

It doesn't stop until the woods are too thick to go any further and it is absolutely spent.

Sliding from the saddle, I turn and slash his other side, sending him crashing back through the trees, hooves pounding.

He'll lead them the wrong way.

But Aisha and Rudi are gone—smoke, hooves, silence. And I'm alone.

# CHAPTER NINE

## *Smoke and Splinters*

Heart hammering, I move through the woods in a crouch, carving a path parallel to the road, back the way we came. A cold sweat clings to my skin.

I emerge in a field behind the cart. From this distance, I can't see inside, but I don't have long. Sooner or later, the men will find the Hucul—abandoned, bleeding—and come looking. I keep low, weaving through long grass and wheat until I reach the road. My pulse pounds in my ears, sweat blurs my vision, and instinct takes over.

Behind the cart now, I catch a glimpse: one occupant. A woman in a brown cloak. Pale as bone, with grey hair plaited down her back. Two Hungarian drafts at the front, whinnying, eager to go. The rear full to overflowing with barrels of food.

I press myself against the wood and ease the talwar free.

Half-crouched, I edge along the cart's side. Through the wheel spokes, I see her scanning the treeline with a brass spyglass. It crosses my mind to shove her out and take the reins—but those hulking thoroughbreds would be on us before I ever climbed out of the dip. And Aisha is still out there.

I dig into that pit of despair where Maria lives and find my rage.

The woman startles when she sees me—spyglass clattering into the cart. Her mouth opens to scream, but I smash the hilt of the talwar into her nose. She slumps back, hands cupping blood, the scream dying on her lips. I don't wait to see what damage I've done. I bend to snatch up the spyglass.

The woman groans and I lift the talwar again to quieten her. Then, I scope the treeline and the fields looking for Aisha, or Rudi. Or anything.

I find the men's horses tied to a pine.

Turning to leave, I follow the woman's eye and find a rifle lay in the cart's footwell. She moves to put a foot on it as I reach down, and she ends up with a fist in her throat.

Back through the field, fast now, rifle in both hands. I cut the churchmen's horses loose and grab the reins, swinging onto the other just as the men break through the trees.

'Stop!'

One man charges, sword flashing. I struggle to turn the horses. Not enough room. The blade comes for my gut—too fast to dodge. I twist, shielding my chest, bracing for pain.

But then—a blur of fur and teeth. Rudi explodes from the grass, snarling, latching onto the man's wrist.

It buys me seconds.

I dig in my heels, gripping tight to the second horse's reins, and thunder back across the field.

At the road, I glance back. The men are running for the cart. No sign of Rudi.

Damn it.

I hate to do it, but I release the second horse and nick its rump. It bolts into the farmland. One less distraction for them—one more chance for me to get away.

The rifle holds one shot.

I swing the horse sideways, line up with the cart, and take aim. The men reach it just as I squeeze the trigger.

The rifle kicks against my shoulder. Smoke curls from the barrel. Both men hit the dirt—but they're up again moments later. I drop the rifle into the long grass and wait.

One of the draft horses tries to bolt. The other staggers, collapses, and doesn't rise. A clean shot, straight to the skull.

The bolting horse jerks the cart sideways, but the weight of the dead horse is too much, and the cart topples, throwing the woman out in the process.

I raise a hand in mock salute to my pursuers, then spur my new horse into a gallop.

It thunders up the rise, hooves devouring the slope. At the crest, out of their line of sight, I pull hard off the road and plunge down a steep bank into a field of tall grass.

The stalks whip at my face, rustling with the breeze, heavy with the sweet, earthy scent of summer. The smell stirs something in me—an ache for home I don't have time to feel.

We charge through the field towards the sound of rushing water. The treeline rises ahead, dark and thick.

The forest swallows us whole.

Tall trees creak overhead like old giants. I lie low against the horse's back, guiding us toward the river's roar. My heart drums against his withers, pulse to pulse.

I glance behind us—nothing but shadows.

Then a clearing. And in it, a vision:

Dati, crouched at the water's edge, fishing for supper.

The memory hits soft and sharp all at once. I almost call out—but then I notice the flask. Always present. Always full.

Was it really there that day? Or has Mama warped my memories to match her bitterness?

The image fades before I can decide.

The horse slows at a rock pool near the base of a small waterfall. The river rushes northward. I look back one last time—just as a blackbird flickers from tree to tree.

No one's behind us.

I dismount and lead the horse to water.

'Drink,' I mutter, voice hoarse.

Kneeling, I refill my flask. My reflection shimmers in the surface: blood-smeared, hair tangled, eyes bruised and swollen.

Grimacing at what I see, I stand and swing back into the saddle.

I follow the river as long as I can. A patch of wild turnips lines the bank—good fortune. Using the talwar and my hands, I dig up as many as I can. The horse gets two. I pocket the rest.

But eventually the river pulls away from the woods, disappearing into terrain I can't navigate. I feed the horse one last turnip, then turn away from the water.

It's time to return to the road. To keep moving. I ride slow, nerves prickling with every crunch of twigs and flap of wings.

Rudi might be out there. Maybe even Aisha.

I can only hope the road hasn't swallowed them too.

I come out from the trees a few miles north, pausing at

the edge to scan the dying daylight.

Nothing moves—just crows and the wind through the grass.

Still, my stomach twists.

I guide the horse forward at a cautious trot, each step towards the open road a battle of will. Part of me wants to turn and vanish into the trees again. But I'd never reach the monastery that way. Not for weeks.

The horse touches gravel. I tighten my grip on the reins until my knuckles turn pale, jaw clenched, every muscle ready to snap.

Nothing happens.

No voices. No riders. No pursuit.

So we go.

Northward, following the winding ribbon of gravel and sand as dusk deepens into night. Miles pass. Distant lights shimmer on the horizon. Maybe a village. Maybe hope.

Then the rifle cracks.

The shot splits the silence like lightning, and the horse screams, staggering sideways in blind panic. We nearly tumble down the slope. Before I can even breathe, a second shot rings out—sharp, clean.

Blood bursts from the horse's shoulder. Claret splashes the air.

All hell breaks loose.

The horse bucks. I'm thrown.

I land hard.

Luck, nothing else, keeps me from hitting a rock. My shoulder takes most of it. My breath's gone, pain lancing through my side. But I'm not dead.

I roll. Rise.

The horse is gone, vanishing into the night with wild

eyes and thundering hooves—and with it, my last chance to ride.

The churchmen ride fast and fresh, closing in.

I don't wait.

I run for the trees, dragging my injured leg.

The tall grass clutches at my boots as I run. My breath rasps, ribs flaring with every step. Behind me, the hooves grow louder. Shouts break through the encroaching dark.

'In the field!'

They come down the slope, torches blazing. Firelight dances across the stalks. I push harder.

Almost there—almost in the trees.

Then a sound.

A snarl.

At first, I think it's a horse. Then I hear the bark. Cold dread floods my limbs.

A hound.

I don't look back—I don't need to.

It hits me like a hammer. Pain erupts in my leg as teeth sink into my calf, and I scream, falling hard. My head hits something cold and unyielding.

Then, darkness.

Hands bound behind my back, ankles tied tight, the churchmen sling me over one of their horses like a sack of meat. One climbs up behind me, jamming his knee into my thigh, then my ribs. No apology. No hesitation. Just violence.

The other mounts his own horse. We head for the road. Towards the waiting wagon.

I strain to lift my head. She's there. The woman. Nose swollen and purple, dried blood crusting her arms. Her mouth twists into a crooked little smile.

'I think it's an improvement,' I rasp, just as she leans over to spit.

'Why didn't you string her up?' she croaks.

'We'll take her with us,' the man behind me says, grabbing a fistful of my hair. He jerks my head back for a better look. 'Hanging's too good for this gypsy bitch.'

'Let me go,' I snarl, twisting, teeth bared, but it's useless.

'Quiet, hag.' He lets go—only to drive a fist into my ribs.

White-hot pain. My breath vanishes. It takes a long time to claw it back.

'I need to find my daughter,' I whimper, braced for more.

'You need to find God,' the crone snaps, reaching down to pluck my rings.

'Your god is no use to me.'

'You're no use to Him.' She drops the rings into a bag. 'But there's a new god in town—and she'll gladly make use of your soul.'

'What does that mean?' I twist, trying to see their faces.

Then, a blow to the back of my head, and everything goes black again.


When I wake, the world is wrong.

Not pain—disorientation. Firelight flickers. Shadows stretch across the dirt. The smell of roasted meat fills the air.

Still slung over the horse, I lie quiet and listen.

'We ride north to the borderlands after we deliver this one,' says one of the men.

I hold my breath.

Their attention shifts. I can feel it like heat on my back.

'Too bad the other bitch escaped.'

'I don't care about the other one,' the woman says, mouth full. 'This one broke my nose. I hope they hang her.'

My heart thunders. I test the ropes. Nothing. But then—I see something at the edge of my vision.

My blade. Sheathed. Strapped to the saddle of the other horse.

A spark of hope.

My feet are bound to the stirrups, hands tied. But if I can move this beast closer...

I drag my legs up as far as the rope and stirrups allow, then jab the gelded thoroughbred with my knee.

He nickers, shifts sideways.

I press flat, eyes shut, praying they don't notice.

A minute passes.

Another kick. A whispered apology.

He shifts again. I can *feel* the other horse now. Close.

One last jab.

My fingers brush leather.

'What's happening?' a voice snaps. 'Is she trying something?'

Boots shuffle through the dirt. A glow gets closer.

'Just the horses,' comes the reply. 'Think they wanna fuck.'

'Don't be filthy,' the crone mutters.

The light fades. Conversation resumes.

I wait—then stretch.

Fingers clawing at nothing, until...

Cold steel.

I draw the talwar with a careful twist of my wrist. Wounds open. Joints cream. My vision pules white. But I've exposed the blade, just a little.

And that's all I need.

Now what?

No leverage. No freedom. And then—a groan slips from

my mouth.

I clamp my jaw and eyes shut.

'What was that?'

'She's out cold,' the woman croaks. 'One last dream before she meets Manette.'

They seem to believe it.

I wait another beat. Then I begin to saw.

The rope is rough. Every second is agony against my wrists. Then—snap.

My hands are free.

But the blade slips and falls between the two animals into the grass.

I freeze.

No sound. No movement.

They haven't noticed.

I wait, burning with cramps and exhaustion, until their voices fade. Until sleep, or silence, swallows them whole.

I ease into a squat, shaking hands gripping the saddle. With one hand, I work at the knot, fingers bleeding against the rope. My other wrist burns from the strain of holding me up.

The knot gives.

I slide down like water. Crouch. Crawl.

My fingers close around the talwar in the grass.

Before sliding it back into its sheath, I cut the rope hitching the two horses to a nearby tree.

I mount one and turn to leave.

But a voice inside stops me.

*They're just going to keep coming.*

*I could end it now. While they sleep.*

My grip tightens on the hilt. I'm about to dismount— then the man stirs, grunting. A log cracks in the fire.

I turn the horse north and ride, leading the second by the reins.

Rain begins just after midnight.

Cold and fine at first, then heavier. It soaks through my clothes, fills my boots, turns the fields to mud. But I don't stop.

Every sound in the dark feels like hooves. Every shadow could be them.

I press on—head down, teeth clenched—urging the horse forward with nothing but grim will and the occasional whispered curse.

The second horse trails behind on a slack lead. I should feel relief—something—but my limbs are numb, and my head's a hive of wasps.

I think of Maria.

Her curls in the morning light. The way she used to hum when she was nervous.

I'll find you, baby. I'll tear the world apart if I have to.

But fear gnaws at the edges of that vow. What if I'm too late?

Rain seeps down my collar and settles like ice in my spine. Every part of me hurts, especially the parts that have to keep going.

Ahead, cornfields stretch off in every direction—dry, broken things hunching like old men waiting to die. But there's a path. And above it, a road winding upwards.

I can't tell if I'm gaining ground or simply delaying the inevitable, but I know one thing: these drays will move faster on stone than sludge.

I urge the horse towards the rise, lying flat against his back, eyes flicking over my shoulder every few seconds, waiting for that wagon to appear.

The road climbs forever, carved black against the bruising edge of dawn. And then I see it.

Light.

Smoke curling from chimney pots like breath.

A hilltop town, hunched and waiting.

Somewhere ahead of me—Maria.

Somewhere behind—monsters in priest's robes.

I chew a few of the nuts Aisha gave me and rub the ache from my wrist. No time for pain. Not yet.

# CHAPTER TEN

## *Stripped to the Bone*

Ravens take flight as I clomp by—cawing and flapping. They scatter from a rabbit carcass and eye me from above, beady and watchful. Two exhausted horses and a woman running on will alone.

Hours pass before I cross a stone bridge into the town. A crooked sign reads Gyor. The air thickens—acrid, clinging to the back of my throat. The whole place reeks, and not a soul stirs.

Hand pressed to my mouth, I dismount. The first house is whitewashed, with a thatched roof and oak-framed windows. A wooden cross is nailed to the door like a warning. I knock. No answer. I try another. And another. Silence.

Then, I sense movement—just ahead. Someone darts between buildings, little more than a shadow. I scramble back into the saddle, heart kicking. I ride forward, but the street is empty. No sound but the horses' hooves and the whisper of running water somewhere nearby.

Deeper into the village, the houses shrink. Stone crumbles. Doors sag on rusted hinges. The polished crosses vanish—replaced by crooked symbols scrawled in chalk and soot. Crude protection.

My arms tremble too much to hold the reins any longer. Hunger rises, claws at my insides as I near the promise of a warm meal. I fall as much as slide from the saddle, bag slung over my aching shoulder, and let the horses wander—let them find water if they can. I can barely keep upright.

The stench thickens. Rancid. Rotted. I gag and stagger as I walk, vision swimming.

Then the bells begin.

Not a peal of welcome, but a single low toll. Again. And again. A sound that rings like a warning through the bones of the town. I don't know whether to cover my ears or my nose.

Doors creak open. People spill into the street like ants from a cracked nest. Gaunt. Dark-eyed beneath the setting sun.

I spin, bewildered.

'Get to the church,' says a long-haired man, passing close. His voice is flat, his eyes hidden beneath a heavy brow. He points with a shovel-sized hand in the direction the crowd flows.

'I need food. And water.'

'Get to the church,' he says again, already gone.

I follow, swept along by the current. The cobbled street opens into a square, where a church squats like an old beast, doors yawning wide. Dozens shuffle inside. Adults. Children.

No one speaks. No one looks back.

I stop at the threshold. Gaze into its cavernous belly. The home of my enemy, I remind myself.

'If you want to see the dawn, you'd best take shelter.' A plump priest brushes my back with his hand as he passes. He moves to usher in the last stragglers, tugging at reins, guiding carts.

Then he reaches to shut the doors.

'Wait.' I lurch forward. Whatever these people fear—I'm in no state to face it alone, and it must be worse than the church itself.

He looks at me sideways, pausing with one hand on the heavy door. I grab the other and help him close it. Together, we drive the bolt home.

'What the hell is going on?' I ask, breath short.

'What the hell indeed,' he mutters.

He takes a lit candle from a table and leads me through the nave. The air inside is thick with wax and sweat. Dozens of people crowd together on the front pews. Children curl in their mothers' arms. Candles flicker on the altar like nervous hearts.

'You are not from here,' he says, voice low. He sets the candle on a bench and turns to me. 'These people have seen horror. Don't expect them to welcome you with a smile.'

'I don't understand.' I scan the hollow belly of the church —the solemn faces, the silence, the way even breath seems sacred. 'From what do we take shelter?'

The priest lifts a bowl from a side table. He shuffles back to the door, trailing droplets of water across the stones.

'From the spawn of hell.'

Ill at ease, I unbuckle my belt and lay the talwar across my lap as I settle into the back pew. The blade's weight is comforting—too comforting. I don't let it go.

The priest walks to the front, head bowed, hands clasped behind his back. A low murmur ripples through the huddled congregation, bunched together on the front rows like sheep before a storm.

At the altar, he looks like a man long defeated by life. Sunken eyes. Wispy hair combed over a balding crown. Shoulders hunched beneath the weight of things he'll never say aloud.

'Lord, have mercy,' he says, voice soft, flat.

'Christ, have mercy,' he continues.

I spot a dark bottle near a small side table, half-hidden in shadow. Claret. A cup sits beside it.

'Lord, have mercy,' he repeats.

I rise, walk to the table, and lift the bottle. It's full, heavy in the hand. I pour, drink deep, and ask myself, *What the fuck am I doing here?*

As I raise the cup again, I pause.

Outside, a snort. A whinny. The priest glances back, eyes sharp now, and I cork the bottle on instinct.

Hooves stomp. Wood creaks. Then the sound shifts— neighing gives way to growling… then screaming.

Then silence.

I step back from the table, bottle in one hand, cup in the other.

'God, the Father in heaven,' the priest mutters, voice rising. 'Have mercy on us all.'

A single thump on the church doors.

Everyone in the room gasps.

Then—stillness.

'Let me in,' comes a voice from outside. Fragile. Frightened. 'Please... you can't leave me out here. I'm all alone in the dark.'

A chill spreads through the church, bleeding into our bones, frosting the breath before our eyes.

I set the wine on the pew beside me and tuck my free hand beneath my arm, glancing at the priest. I want answers. What I get is fear.

A ragged man stands. Tousled hair. Grey beard. His face is drawn and blotched with fatigue. Others around him reach out, tug at his arms, whisper desperate warnings.

'It's no use,' they say, pulling him back.

But he shoves them off. Keeps moving.

'Please don't,' someone sobs.

'I can't leave her out there,' he says, tears streaking his cheeks. 'Lucille?'

'Papa?' The voice outside again. Higher now. Childlike.

He stops.

'Papa, don't leave me out here. I'm begging you.'

Another man—a wall of muscle and fury—rises from a pew, stepping into his path.

'Sit down, Karl.'

Karl doesn't break stride. 'You know I can't do that.'

'You'll kill us all.'

They collide in the aisle—shoulders crashing, fists grasping for purchase. Karl is wiry but wild, thrashing like a man with nothing left to lose. The larger man stumbles, off-balance for a heartbeat, tripping on the hem of his own coat.

Karl thrusts a knee into the big man's gut, toppling him, then surges forward, stepping over him, eyes locked on the door.

'Karl.' The priest descends from the altar, a trembling

hand raised like a frail dam against floodwater. 'That is not your Lucille out there. You know it as well as I. That is the devil in disguise. A trick to lure you to your death.'

'Perhaps... she can be returned to herself.'

I don't know what waits beyond that door. But I see the horror carved into these people's faces. I see what they've lost. And I see myself in Karl. Grief driving every step. The world falling away, leaving only the need to act—to fight, even if it means dying.

And I know—for certain—that I don't want him to open that door.

I free my weapon. Unfasten the top buttons of my coat.

If he moves, I'll stop him.

'Your daughter is already with our Lord,' the priest says, voice cracking. 'What you hear is nothing but a cruel deception. A manipulation, meant to drag you into the dark.'

'Pray with me, Karl,' he pleads. 'Pray for all the lost children.'

Karl collapses to his knees, his whole body trembling. His breath clouds the air in ragged gasps.

'Still as weak as ever, Papa?' The girl's voice shifts—no longer frightened, but cruel. Wicked. 'Such a shame. But I'm sure someone inside desires what we have to offer.'

'Ignore her,' the priest snaps. 'Stay seated. Pray.'

'There are four of us,' comes another voice—silken, strange. 'Alone in the cold. We only want a little company. Someone kind. Someone warm.'

A third voice joins, lilting and low: 'Come share the dark with us. We'll make you feel needed.'

The priest raises his cross with a shaking hand and steps towards the door, robes swaying. 'Be gone, demons,' he commands. 'Flee from the house of God.'

Laughter answers him. Not from four voices—but from dozens. A rising tide of women's laughter surrounding the church on all sides.

'How 'bout it, priest?' one voice teases. 'Come outside and be reborn into eternal life.'

The frost spreads deeper, prickling at the skin, numbing the breath in our lungs.

I want to move—to act—but I'm rooted to the pew. My mind returns to Aisha's house. The dhampir. The whispering darkness.

I glance at the townsfolk. Hollow-eyed. Gaunt. Their faces are maps of suffering. The only fire left here is in Karl, now pacing the aisle, muttering and cursing, grief spurring him on.

The priest stands firm at the threshold, cross lifted high, spine bowed beneath the weight of fear. If a fight breaks out tonight, it won't be against monsters—it'll be with those trying to reach the door.

Then—silence. The voices outside fall away like wind dying in the trees.

I rise and cross to the priest.

'They have my daughter,' I whisper. 'Tell me what you know.'

His jowls tremble. He nods.

'What happened here?'

He gestures to the huddled crowd near the front pews. 'It happened quickly. Just weeks ago, this town was full to bursting.' His voice breaks. A tear streaks down his face. 'Now... we're all that's left.'

I do a quick count—twenty-seven. 'This can't be everyone.'

'Men, women and children, taken from their homes in

the night.' He lifts a hand limply to wipe his brow. 'Some of the men have found their way back, only to be reduced to dust by the morning sun.'

My chest tightens. 'The sun burns them?'

He nods. 'I wouldn't believe it if I hadn't seen it with my own eyes.'

'What about the children?'

He shakes his head. 'They return also.'

A flicker of rage burns across his grieving face. 'They're outside. They haunt this town. Night after bloody night.'

'Spellbound?'

'No.' His tone drops like a blade. 'It's darker than that. What you hear out there—what you *think* are your children —those are creatures of hell. There is nothing left of what they were.'

'How can you know this?'

'I saw one of them tear the flesh from a man's bones. He screamed for mercy. They felt nothing. No pity. No soul.'

'Jesus.'

He nods once. 'Indeed.'

I lean against the cold wall, trying to steady my thoughts. 'There must be others taking shelter in this town. This can't be everybody.'

'This is the last church standing. The others are ash and bones.'

'They burned them?'

'And everyone inside.'

I crouch, breath shallow. My head reels.

'At first... I thought I could save them.' He shuts his eyes, exhales long and slow. 'I walked the streets. At night. In the name of the Lord.'

'You *faced* them?' I lean in, stunned.

'Me and my faith. That's all I had.'

He glances at Karl, then back to me as I rise from the frost creeping beneath the door.

'I didn't save anyone. But the cross—' He touches it reverently. 'It saved me. They recoiled. Squirmed. It was painful for them.'

'They fear the Lord?'

'More than fear. They *feel* it. And they cannot enter a holy place like this.'

'So, they burn them?' My mouth dries.

'An evening's entertainment,' he says bitterly. 'Slaughtering the faithful.'

I clutch my stomach and fold forward. The thought of Maria —snatched away by those monsters—brings a rush of dizziness that nearly topples me. And the image of being burned alive, like the others... my heart hammers to escape my ribs.

'None have come back safe?' I whisper, swallowing bile.

The priest only shakes his head.

My legs give out and I fold. Vomit spills between my boots, stringing from my lips as the world tilts, spins, collapses in on itself.

The priest leaves without a word.

When he returns, he's holding a chipped cup of water— and a look that cuts deeper than pity. It's disappointment.

'When I saw your weapons,' he says, 'there was a moment I considered barring you from this place.'

He hands me the cup. I drink without meeting his eye.

'I came here to find my daughter,' I murmur. 'But I see now—all hope is gone.'

As if summoned by my words, a chant rises outside.

Low. Rhythmic. It coils around the church like a snake around the neck.

Burn. Burn. Burn.

The congregation stirs—gasps, clutches blankets and coats. Eyes dart to the doors.

'The time is upon us,' the priest says, but there's iron in his voice now. 'Follow me.'

He hurries to the altar. People scramble to their feet, bundling belongings, lifting children, clutching loaves and water jars. No screaming. No chaos. Just practiced dread.

I push myself upright, curiosity overtaking nausea. My legs tremble but hold.

At the altar, the priest and another man roll back the blood-red carpet, revealing a trapdoor in the stone floor. The priest grabs a bowl, fills it with holy water from the font, and hurries to the nave. The other man lifts the heavy hatch.

Hinges scream, but one by one, the townsfolk descend.

The priest works in frantic loops—drenching doorways, pews, and flagstones with the water. A ritual of desperation. Of faith. Of fear.

But not hope. Not for me.

Even if we live through the night… how am I supposed to face what waits above?

He catches my eye. 'Go.'

Outside, the chanting rises to a frenzy. Burn, burn, burn. The windows glow —orange tongues licking at the glass.

I don't hesitate.

I check my hip for my weapon, grab the church wine, and drop through the trapdoor. Down the ladder, past another hatch, into darkness.

The tunnel swallows me whole.

The walls are limestone—cold, pale, and slick in the

candlelight. I hear the heavy door slam shut above, then the grind of a bolt. The priest descends after, pausing to seal the second hatch before joining us.

'Keep moving,' the priest calls, and the congregation shuffles forward, parting just enough for him to push through to the front.

I stay at the back, heart beating like the kick of a mule.

The tunnel is silent but for footfalls and breath. Then the smell of smoke comes—thin at first, a ghost of fire drifting in behind us. No one speaks of it. We all feel it.

Eventually, the priest raises a hand. We stop.

We're deep into the tunnel now—so deep the ladder is lost to darkness, the hatch far behind. Ahead lies nothing but black.

The priest has an emergency stash, I realise, as the townsfolk pass around blankets, shawls, cloaks. They settle into the stone like ghosts returned to the crypt.

I make my way to the front.

'Where does it lead?' I ask.

'Edge of the forest,' he says, staring into the dark. His voice is calm. Hardened. 'Barred from both ends—from the inside. They won't reach us here.'

'You're sure?'

He turns, meets my gaze. 'I still cling to hope, child.' A beat. Then he raises his voice to the others. 'As you should.'

The gaunt faces turn to face him. Eyes sunken, skin pale, mouths silent.

'Those who hope in the Lord will renew their strength,' he says softly. 'They will soar on wings like eagles, run and not grow weary. They will walk and not be faint.'

He looks back at me. 'Let faith guide us in this time of desperation. Let hope be our strength.'

I scoff—quiet but bitter.

'If you knew what I've done,' I say, 'you wouldn't speak to me of faith. Or hope.'

I turn, walking deeper into the tunnel until the smell of smoke fades, worried breaths die out, and the candlelight is naught but the distant glow of spirits.

Then I sit, knees to my chest, weapon across my lap.

'You'll be my blanket,' I mutter, raising the wine bottle to my lips.

I drink. And drink. The priest's voice still rattling in my skull—nothing remains of what they once were.

I press my forehead to my knees. Tears come hot and fast. 'Maria,' I whisper. The name breaks me. 'Please don't let it be true. Please. Please.'

I see her face. Her curls. The tiny scar on her chin. That little yellow ribbon she never let me tie straight. I think of the priest—the dead one—the one I murdered. 'I'm sorry,' I whimper. 'Please, punish me, not her.'

Then I see Luca's face. His steady hands. His gentleness. My Luca. My love. My ally.

'They don't deserve this,' I whisper into the dark.

'Have no fear,' comes the voice beside me.

I flinch.

The priest again—stooped, gentle.

'Their evil cannot reach us down here.'

'I'm not afraid,' I lie.

He glances at the wine in my hand. 'That bottle says otherwise.'

I look down at it. Shrug. Pass it over.

He takes a long drink, then hands it back.

'I blame you not,' he says, still stooped. 'Theft is a way of life for your kind, I suppose.'

He hesitates. Then, softer, 'But I've seen worse from my own.'

I lift an eyebrow. 'And I don't blame you, Father.'

He tilts his head, bemused.

'Believing everything you're told without question—requisite for the job, I suppose.'

A rustle and mutter ripple through the gathered townsfolk. The priest rises, turns to settle them.

'Be calm,' he says. 'We don't want to draw attention.'

Then he turns back and lowers himself beside me, settling onto the stone with a sigh.

'My people are men and women of trade.' I think of Luca's bowls—how lovingly he carved each curve. Devel, they were beautiful. 'Woodworkers, mostly. Keeps us close to the forest, which I've always been grateful for.'

The air thickens with the smell of old wood burning. The crowd shifts, uneasy.

'We've stone masons too,' I say, locking eyes with the priest. 'Their work stands long after we're driven out of the towns that paid for it. And jewellers—our rings still grace the fingers of those who spat on our names.'

I lean back against the stone, voice colder now. 'To be Romani is to be cursed to outstay your welcome. To be useful... and despised for it.'

The priest nods slowly. 'And you? What's your trade?'

'Hunting,' I say, a small, bitter smile tugging at my mouth. 'My dati taught me. His dati taught him. But I'm the last. The line ends with me.'

'And now you hunt those who took your daughter.'

He reaches for my arm. I flinch away.

'They took my husband too,' I whisper. Then, voice rising, 'And the church helped them do it.'

The priest stiffens, wrestling with the weight of what I've just laid at his feet. 'Even the most devout may be... compromised, I suppose.'

'Compromised?' I echo, and my gaze falls to the crucifix at his chest.

He follows my stare. 'No man lives up to *His* standard. Not one. There's good and evil in all of us.'

I take another drink. 'Lately I've seen more evil than good.'

He gestures vaguely upward. 'Those monsters out there were wives once. Daughters. Mothers. They'd rip me to pieces without hesitation—but that doesn't erase what they once were. Not in the eyes of God.'

'And if the bad outweighs the good?'

'Then blessed are we that there's still time to tip the scale. And you—' he narrows his eyes, studying me '—you're a formidable woman.'

'That's what frightens me,' I mutter. 'There's nothing I wouldn't do for Maria.'

He rests a hand on my shoulder. 'That love is a gift. But I think you have other gifts too. Use them well. You'll do alright.'

I say nothing. I don't believe him.

Smoke curls stronger through the tunnel. My stomach knots.

'When did you last eat?'

'Don't worry about me,' I say, but my gut growls like thunder.

'It's not much,' comes a voice from the dark.

A pale woman offers bread and cheese with a trembling hand. Green eyes. White hair.

'You should eat,' she says.

I nod, take the food, but my appetite's gone. My mouth's too dry to chew.

'You'll need strength to get her back,' the priest says. 'And maybe sleep.'

A dry laugh slips past my lips. 'Not much chance of that.'

I take the wine and the food, shuffle deeper into the darkness, away from the others.

*Nothing remains of what they once were.* That's what he said.

I close my eyes and whisper into the dark. 'Please don't let that be true.'

Maria's face floats before me—so alive it hurts to look, and I drink—not to forget, but to keep from falling apart.

Something crashes overhead, and the townsfolk shriek. Then murmur, shift. A child cries in the dark.

And I let it hold me. The weight of it all. The odds very much stacked against me.

I curl tighter in the dark, talwar laid across my lap like a grave marker. The wine bottle pressed to my side like a relic. Chewing the bread in silence.

And I wait.

For morning. For death. For nothing at all.

# CHAPTER ELEVEN

## *No More Waiting*

Clang.

The sound rings down the tunnel like a scream—metal on metal, distant but unmistakable.

The first hatch.

The breath in the tunnel stills. The murmurs die. Only the crackle of a dying candle remains. Somewhere in the dark, a child whimpers.

The second clang brings stifled screams and hands clamped over mouths.

That's when I rise.

Each clang against the hatch is like a knife twisting in my belly, and something breaks in me.

Not a bone. Not the last piece of hope snapping quietly in the dark.

This is bigger. Hotter. A shattering dam.

They're coming.

And these people—the priest, the townsfolk—they would wait here to die?

Wait while monsters rip through stone and fire to tear us apart?

No.

They already took Maria. They don't get to take me too. Not like this. Not curled up in a pit like a rat.

Fists clenched, jaw set, I draw my weapon and start back to the hatch. Condensation drips from the stone above as I push my way through the shuffling crowd of locals.

The priest stirs.

'What are you doing?' he asks, scurrying after me with a flickering candle in hand.

'If they break through,' I say, 'I want to be here to meet them.'

Worried faces gather around him as the clanging continues overhead. Each jolt brings a flinch, a cry.

Dismissing his words with a swipe of my hand, I turn away and continue until the banging stops, replaced by the submissive shriek of the hinges.

'They're through the first door,' someone screams, starting a mad scramble to the other end of the tunnel.

'You can't face them,' the priest tells me. 'Not alone.'

I turn to face him, my face as hard as these stone walls. 'You people can cower here behind your God, but if I'm going to die tonight, I'll do it on my own terms.'

'It must be almost dawn.' He risks a glance back into the darkness. 'We can escape into the forest, outrun them 'til sunrise.'

Another thud above. Then scraping boots on the ladder. The second door is ripped open.

Pale light spills down through the hatch, casting weak shadows onto the stone. A man drops into the tunnel, a silhouette against the smoke-stained dawn.

He lunges forward with a short blade in his hand, and I swing my steel, meeting his with a ring. The sword falls out of his grip, and I slash upwards, cutting through flesh with sickening ease.

The man wails.

And falls.

At the other end of the tunnel, people scramble to the other hatch, shoving and clambering over each other. Screaming. Groaning. Fighting amongst themselves.

Another figure drops down the ladder—fast, blade in hand—but he's barely touching stone when I cut him down. The steel finds his gut. He shrieks, collapses. Hits the floor with a thud and doesn't get up.

The tunnel reeks of blood and guts as it dawns on me—

These aren't monsters.

These are men.

Like Luca.

I feel sick. Darkness creeps in at the edge of my vision.

Behind me, the other hatch screams open.

I stumble backwards, blade slick, breath ragged. The walls seem to pulse with heat and panic. Someone sobs on the ground as I make my way to the escape. A dropped candle flickers nearby, throwing contorted shadows against the stone.

I press a blood-slick hand to the wall to steady myself.

I'm alone in the tunnel, but for the sobbing woman.

Above, the hatch gapes.

I hesitate. Reach for the woman crouched against the stone. Then a third man drops into the tunnel.

Planting my back foot, I raise the talwar as he rushes at me.

His blade is arched like a bow, glinting in the candlelight.

I brace myself, hold my breath. Then, slash. He cuts the woman's throat without slowing.

I stagger back, shocked. Clatter into the ladder.

He comes on, blade bloodied. Swings.

I parry.

Steel slashes past my face, beds itself in one of the wooden rungs.

And I nick his thigh.

He releases his grip, clamps his hands over his leg as blood spurts free.

'You shouldn't have done that,' I say, pointing the tip of my weapon at the dead woman.

He groans, legs giving out. And I open his belly.

A gasp passes his dying lips as he tries, and fails, to speak.

I glance up at the light. Pale and cold. Too clean for this place.

But I won't wait for it to be swallowed by fire.

I sheath the talwar, grip the rungs, and climb.

Not to flee.

But to face whatever waits above.


I breach the hatch and emerge amongst the trees just as the first screams reach my ears. Not sharp or sudden—but low and ragged, the kind that comes from people who've already been crying too long.

Through the shifting veil of smoke, I see them—villagers. Dozens of them. Dirty, hunched, stumbling like cattle. Driven from the trees, through the church graveyard, and into the village square beyond by men on horseback, who shout and crack whips that snap like lightning. The horses snort and rear, hooves pounding the soft ground, sending up a storm of earth and ash.

The smell of scorched wood rides the wind—sharp, acrid, bitter. It clings to my skin, curls through my clothes, seeps into my mouth like something rotting. The air is thick with it, heavy and hot in my lungs. I raise a sleeve over my face, but it barely helps.

Each cough from the crowd cuts through the morn—wet, rattling, broken. Children cry out—thin, wheezing wails. One woman stumbles and goes down, arms wrapped around a bundle I pray is still breathing. A thrall leaps from his mount, strikes her with the flat of a blade, and hauls her back to her feet like a sack of grain.

The smouldering wreck of the church looms ahead, skeletal and blackened, its charred beams jutting from the smoke like ribs from a corpse. Flames still twitch in the ruins —red tongues licking at collapsed walls, feeding on what little remains.

And then—movement. A different shape, lower to the ground.

My eyes catch a figure crouched behind a fallen tree. Robes dirtied with soot, a glint of metal at his chest.

The priest.

Clutching the bark like it's the only thing holding him to this world. His eyes are wild, unblinking, locked on the mounted men herding his flock like beasts.

I wait. Still. Listening.

The crack of a whip.

A muffled sob.

A shout—foreign words barked with venom.

127

I wait until the thralls are distracted, their attention turned to a wagon being loaded in the square. Then I move. Low to the earth, fast and silent, my boots skating over pine needles and soot. The smoke stings my eyes, tears stream down my face—but I don't stop until I'm beside him, hidden in the shadow of the fallen tree.

'We need to do something,' I whisper.

The priest doesn't answer. His eyes are glazed, staring past me into the smoke and ruin.

'Are you hearing me?' I grip his shoulder and shake. He blinks, finally sees me.

'They're all dead,' he says flatly.

'No.' I thrust my talwar forward, streaked with blood, and point towards the blackened church ruins. 'Those were no vampyres. They bled too easily. They screamed.'

I glance back at the square. 'Your people can still be saved. But they'll come looking for the ones I killed—it's only a matter of time. We strike now, or not at all.'

He doesn't answer, so I leave him behind and crawl forward, low and fast across the forest floor, until I reach the treeline.

From here, the scene is clearer. The villagers are herded like animals, ringed by figures that they once called family or friend. Most carry clubs or rusted swords, but many are unarmed—men with cold, unblinking eyes—barking orders.

The ruined church still breathes smoke. Its rafters groan, half-eaten by fire. Flames flicker red and orange against the ash-streaked sky. The heat licks my skin even from here.

Children wail. Mothers sob. The men stay silent. One by one, they're shoved into a waiting cart—old wood, iron-bound. A prison on wheels.

And then—movement. A wiry man, gaunt as a plucked

bird, breaks from the huddle and bolts for the trees.

My breath catches. I sink low. The priest appears beside me, eyes sharp now, jaw clenched.

We watch the runner. He's fast but desperate, weaving like a wounded deer. Hope flickers—then dies.

A brute barrels after him. No weapon. Just size. He slams into the man from behind, driving him to the ground with bone-jarring force.

'Let me go!' the man shrieks, flailing like a fish on a hook. But the brute doesn't speak. Just mounts him, raises his fists —and begins to punch.

Once. Twice. Again.

Flesh gives. Blood spatters. The crowd wails, but no one moves. Blow after blow crushes the man's face into the dirt.

The brute lifts him by the arm—barely conscious—and hurls him into a mound of loose stones. Then, smiling, he turns and hoists a slab the size of a coffin lid to his chest.

I grip my talwar, heart racing.

'I can't—' I start to rise.

The priest's hand clamps my arm. 'There's nothing the two of us can do,' he hisses.

'No,' someone screams from the villagers. 'Please stop!'

The broken man raises one arm in a feeble shield.

The stone falls.

Crunch. A wet, snapping sound. The man's arm folds like paper. The second blow splits his skull open. His face turns towards me, half-gone, unseeing. Blood pours into the earth like wine from a shattered bottle.

A hush descends. No sound but the ragged weeping of three children.

I can't breathe.

'We can't leave them,' I whisper.

And then I see it-the cart, waiting on the far side of the square. The hag sits up front, and with her, the two churchmen.

The priest follows my gaze. 'It's unforgivable,' he gasps, spitting the word like it burns.

He lets go of my arm.

I raise the talwar, my knuckles white on the hilt.

We lock eyes. Nod.

And I charge forwards.

The scream that leaves my mouth isn't mine. It belongs to something deeper — older. A mother. A widow. A hunter.

The brute turns as I close the gap, swinging a fist the size of a shovel. But my blade is faster. It sings through the air, meets his knuckles, and keeps going—splitting his hand to the wrist.

He howls, drops back, clutching the ruined mess of his hand.

I spin. Black cloak, silver blade. One smooth arc.

The talwar finds his throat. And he finds his end.

He drops to his knees, gurgling. Blood bubbles from his mouth and neck. Still, he tries to stand, staggering forward on instinct.

Then he falls.

The next two rush me. One's a farmer—bare hands, wild eyes. The other wears monk's robes, but he holds a soldier's sword.

The farmer charges—no weapon, no caution, just a desperate howl and flailing limbs. I parry left and bring the talwar around with both hands, cutting through his belly in a clean, brutal arc. He folds with a sickening cry, clutching his spilling guts as he drops into a heap at my feet.

The soldier strikes before the blood even hits the ground.

I see the blade—but I'm too slow. Twisting on my heel saves the arm, but not the leg. The sword kisses my thigh, tearing fabric, flesh. I howl, stumble, but stay upright.

He thrusts again—quick, measured.

This time, I'm ready.

I step sideways, feel the wind of the blade pass my ribs, and respond with a flurry.

The talwar slashes across his neck, his cheek, his chest. He drops the sword and raises his arms too late.

I drive the blade into his ribs, feel it punch between them, feel the resistance give way. He collapses to his knees, blood soaking the front of his robe.

Over his shoulder, I catch a glimpse of movement—three small forms slipping into the trees, the priest guiding them.

Then I'm not alone.

The townsfolk are fighting back—grappling, swinging fists, wrestling for weapons. One woman drives her elbow into a captor's throat. A child throws a rock with all the fury of the world behind it.

But my next challenge is already closing in.

Four come for me now—two hulking bastards, one wielding a maul, the other a lance. Beside them, two leaner men fan out, blades drawn, eyes cold.

They circle like dogs scenting blood.

Then—another flash of robes from the woods. The priest reappears, shouting Bible verse as he faces a brute of a man.

And I'm still surrounded.

This might be it. My last fight.

I think of Maria, of Luca. Of Mama's weathered hands, her rough lullabies. I whisper a prayer—not for salvation, but for them. Let them be safe. Let them be far from this.

The first strike comes.

The lance thrusts for my face. A sword whistles behind me.

I don't know how I sense it—only that I do. Instinct or something older. Older than fear. Older than me. The gift Dati talked of. His gift to me.

I duck.

The lance misses. I bat it aside and roll away from the sword just as it slices the air behind me. Straight into the path of the maul.

It comes down like thunder.

I swing up, cleave into the brute's thigh. Bone splits. He drops, howling, clutching his leg.

Another sword comes for me.

I twist—slash low. My blade finds an ankle and lays it open.

The lance hisses past again.

The air fills with steel. With shouts and curses. With blood.

I duck. Roll. Turn.

I gasp, sweat stinging my eyes, my grip white-knuckled on the talwar. Every limb screams. I've lost count of the wounds. The pain. I only know I'm slowing. Too slow.

Another joins the fray. Rapier in hand, lean and snarling.

He stabs. Slashes. Curses. I dodge, barely. One cut grazes my arm. Another tears my coat.

But I can't last.

My arms are stone. My legs quake. There's no rhythm now. Only survival. Only breath.

The rapier finds its mark.

Pain erupts in my shoulder—white-hot, blinding. The blade hits bone and keeps going. I scream. Drop to one knee.

The world narrows. The sounds blur.

I'm down. Surrounded. I feel the end coming.

They close in. Maul raised. Swords lifted.

One heartbeat.

Two.

I grip the talwar in both hands. One last surge. One last swing.

The blade bites. Cuts through a wrist like twine.

A hand drops beside me.

The man screams. I scream louder.

I'm still here.

Ducking the sword meant to take off my head, I fall back, blind with pain, breath ragged. My shoulder's on fire. The maul comes down like judgement.

I wrench the rapier from my flesh with a scream and roll, just as the blow shatters stone where my skull was a moment ago.

Another sword hisses down, missing me by a breath.

Three of them now. Looming. Bloodied. Unstoppable.

Weapons rise.

The end is coming.

Then—something happens.

A wet thunk, and the swordsman's throat bursts open. An arrowhead replaces his Adam's apple. He stares in stunned silence, then drops his sword, clutching at the shaft.

The others turn—too slow.

Rudi crashes into them like a beast unchained. A blur of teeth and fury. One man vanishes beneath him, buried in snarls and arterial spray.

I lurch upright, talwar barely gripped in numb fingers. From the corner of my eye, I spot her—Aisha. Thundering towards us on horseback, hair streaming, face like stone.

I plant my feet, ready to strike, but the last two attackers flee—limping, bloody, scrambling to the cart with the churchmen and the bitch.

The horses lurch forward at the crack of the whip, and the cart rattles off, dust and blood trailing behind.

Aisha reins in beside me.

'You alright?' she asks.

'I'll live,' I say, though my legs betray me.

She reaches over her shoulder and pulls one of those strange arrows from her quiver.

She sets the fuse aflame, nocks the arrow, draws, and looses it skyward.

It sails.

Lands in the cart bed.

I suck in a breath to curse—but the world erupts.

The cart detonates in a thunderclap of fire and metal. A shockwave knocks me back a step. The horses scream, tear free of the burning wreck, and gallop off through the village.

Inside the cart, flames lick up the walls as the men scream.

'Shit.' My eyes find the burning torso of the woman, and I smile.

Aisha swings down from the saddle and gives me a once-over.

'How'd you find me?' I ask.

She smirks, brushing dirt from her sleeve as the townsfolk surround us, dazed and bloodied.

'I followed the mess you left behind.'

I manage a smile—crooked, heavy. The kind that comes after too much pain and too little sleep. My legs tremble beneath me. My hands throb.

I look out across the smouldering, blood-soaked ruin, eyes burning as they land on the priest. He kneels in the ash, hands limp at his sides. A man broken, not by violence—but by what he couldn't prevent.

Then the pain returns. All at once.

My knees buckle. The ground doesn't rush up—it tilts sideways. I crash into it. Cold and gritty beneath my palms.

Blood pulses from the ragged hole in my shoulder—hot, steady, rhythmic. Each heartbeat slams through me like a hammer on stone. The world shrinks. Light bleeds. My vision tunnels, colour draining until everything is grey and red.

Aisha's voice cuts through the haze, sharp but far away.

She's kneeling beside me, her hand hot on my shoulder.

'You've lost a lot of blood.'

I try to answer, but my tongue is thick. My lips won't form words.

Everything blurs. Frayed at the edges.

And then the dark folds over me—soft as velvet, heavy as earth.


Light creeps in.

I wake with a groan—shoulder burning, mouth full of soot and iron.

The air reeks of stale ale and old wood-smoke.

I blink, slow and dazed.

I'm in a tavern, stretched out on a table like it's my wake.

The room is still.

Quiet in that way that makes your skin itch—like the world is holding its breath.

No footsteps. No voices. Just the tick of cooling wood and the hush of death.

I squint into the gloom, eyes adjusting to the light filtering through dirt-smeared windows.

I try to sit, but pain lances from my leg to my shoulder—

sharp enough to make me bite my tongue. The snagging pull of fresh stitches.

A figure stirs in the corner — Aisha.

She doesn't startle. Just rises slowly, like the dawn.

'You're awake,' she says, coming to me.

I nod, though it takes a moment to find my voice. 'Where is everyone?'

'Gone.' Her boots make no sound on the wooden floor. 'They had the sense to flee hours ago. Took what they could. Headed for the pass.'

'Rudi?'

'Outside. Keeping watch.'

I nod. 'You stayed?'

'I wasn't leaving you.'

She leans over me, checking the bandage on my leg, her tattooed fingers brushing the dressing. Then my shoulder.

'How are you still breathing?'

'Maria,' I rasp, my mouth dry as bone. 'I'll never stop until—'

'I know.'

She squeezes my hand — warm and steady. 'Dusk is fast approaching. And we must not be here when it comes.'

'Where do you want to go?' I glance around for my weapon among the detritus.

'We ride west. I know a safe place. We'll shelter for a few nights.'

I push myself upright — pain flashing white-hot in my shoulder and chest. 'Maria might not have a few nights.'

'I've sent word to the others. They'll meet us there.'

'No.' I try to stand. The pain floors me. 'I can't—'

'Impatience is dangerous, Nura.' She steadies me. 'You're injured, untrained. You can't face even one vampyre alone, let alone a nest.'

'You still doubt me?'

'Nura, you would have died today if I hadn't arrived.'

I scoff as she slips an arm around me and helps me to my feet.

'Patience is bitter,' she says softly. 'But its fruit is sweet.'

I twist away from her, pain ripping through my thigh.

'Death is bitter. Loss is bitter. Saving Maria—and killing those fucking monsters—that is sweet.'

'The only hope we have to save Maria is to strike when we're strongest. That means waiting. For the others. For daylight. For you to heal.'

I close my eyes. Breathe through the pain. Stay upright.

'Two days,' I mutter. Bitter—not at her. At myself. At this body that won't keep up with what I need it to do.

Aisha comes to me again, supporting me with those steady, tattooed hands.

'What you want to do… I don't think anyone could do it. Not alone.'

She leads me outside. A single horse waits. Rudi licks my fingers as I limp past.

'They were thralls?' I ask, glancing at the charred cart, the ruined bodies.

She lowers to help me into the stirrup.

'The churchmen, I don't think so. The others…' she scans the mess of body parts and rubble.

'To stay with the ones you love—wouldn't you do anything? If the choice was that, or death? That, or never seeing your child again?'

'I couldn't slaughter my own people.'

'They chose servitude. Slavery. For the chance to glimpse someone they loved—just once more. They didn't abandon them. No matter the cost.'

'How?'

'One taste of vampyre blood is all it takes to relinquish free will.'

She pulls a flask from the saddlebag and hands it to me. I drink.

My chest tightens as the fight replays in my mind.

'They would have killed you,' Aisha says quietly, reading my silence.

'You don't understand.' I turn away. 'We *slaughtered* them. Not vampyres, but men. Fathers. *Husbands.*'

'As they would have slaughtered you.'

She kneels beside me, warm hand resting on mine. 'To set them free is a gift.'

I stare at my hands. Still red. Still shaking. Not from fear.

But from the thrill of it—the clean, hot rush of killing an enemy.

'Is that what it takes?' I whisper. 'To win?'

'To survive,' Aisha replies.

She slips her shoulder under me and shoves me up into the saddle.

A scream tears loose as my leg swings over.

And then we ride west—into the bleeding light, the sun dragging the day down behind it. Not away from Maria exactly. Just the long way round.

# CHAPTER TWELVE

## *Blood That Burns*

Aısha's horse is majestic, carrying us both with ease. Me at the back, Aisha holding the reins. We wind our way out through the empty streets, past toppled carts and abandoned homes. Smoke clinging to the air like a wet blanket.

Rudi comes and goes, chasing ghosts in and out of buildings, before falling in beside us again. That dog has seen too much. Things no beast should witness, but still he stays.

'No stops,' Aisha tells me. 'We must arrive before nightfall. They travel fast and will be looking for us.'

I tap her side to say I understand. That I know what follows us. That I fear it. That I fear myself.

West takes us down a steep slope as we leave Gyor behind, and each step, each jolt, brings a jarring pain to my shoulder that radiates to my fingertips and up to my teeth.

But I swallow it to keep the agony from passing my lips and slowing us down.

When we hit level ground, Aisha turns and flashes me a look, then puts the mare into a thunderous gallop. And I'm sure I'll die on this horse's back—or beneath its hooves.

A gold and red headscarf holds Aisha's hair in place, but mine whips about my face and I almost fall, swiping it from my eyes. She somehow notices my troubles and slows to loosen a ribbon from her wrist.

'Tie it back.'

She waits just a moment for me to fasten my hair, and then we're off again, rushing past fields and farms with the sinking sun bleeding out across the horizon.

'You're right about something.' Aisha twists just enough to look back at me, her voice raised over the wind. 'There's no better feeling than killing those monsters.'

I open my mouth to speak, but before I can respond, she continues.

'With your abilities, you could become a true vampyre hunter. A name whispered in fear, but you need training. Need to learn how to control your fear.'

'I'm not afraid,' I spit.

'Yes, you are.' She slows the horse a little as we come to a bridge. 'I can hear it in your voice. Feel it in your touch. See it in the way you fight.'

'That's a mother's anger. They should fear me.'

Aisha smiles at that. 'When you've seen the blackness in their hearts and the merciless pits of their eyes. When you've witnessed people being seduced and fed upon willingly, you will wish you had more time. More training.'

She doesn't shout or spit her words at me. Her voice is calm, but the pain in her eyes is unmissable, as is the tremble in her hands.

'You're right,' I tell her, doing my best to suppress the images blooming in my mind of Maria and Luca being bled.

'You have other gifts,' she adds. 'The way you avoided their blows—that's something special.'

I take a breath, hesitant to dig in to such topics, but in the end, anything that can help me get my family back is worth exploring.

'Sometimes, I feel things before I see them. Like the air folds different when I'm in danger.'

The wind might've stolen my words, but I speak on anyway. 'Dati used to say I had the sight—same as him, same as his dati. That I'd see danger before it came.'

Aisha nods. 'I've heard of such things.'

'He died before I could learn to control it.'

'Then we must work on it together. He would want you to wield his gift.'

With every jolt, my grip slips. Not just from the saddle— from everything. 'Do you have a family?'

'A long time ago.'

She shakes her head, turning her attention back to the road as we come over the arching bridge and onto a track.

'When I get my family back, we're leaving this place for good. That was always the plan—and still is.'

I just pray I'm not too late.


We follow the track until it's little more than a thinning of grass, the path behind us swallowed whole by darkness.

Ahead, the western mountain range rises like broken teeth. Storm clouds bunch above the peaks, and rain drifts in —first a mist, then heavy as thrown nails.

'Down there,' Aisha says, pointing towards a dip in the

fields.

A stone house sits nestled among rows of vineyards that stretch in every direction, disappearing into the foothills. A wide gravel path cuts through the vines to a stone house, flanked by two outbuildings.

We stable the horse out back, then hurry for the door just as lightning tears the sky open. We burst inside, soaked and breathless. The dark interior greets us with nothing but silence.

No one's home.

'They should be here by now,' Aisha murmurs, shedding her wet cloak. Her face is pinched, her voice quieter than I've ever heard it. 'Something's not right.'

Night sinks deeper into the walls. Aisha grows restless, slipping in and out of the main room.

'What are you doing?' I ask as she returns with arms full of wood.

'We need warmth.'

She builds a small fire, lighting it with a striker and flint, as I stew in the aromas of the herbs hanging above our heads, dried beyond use.

As the flames warm the room, we sit on opposite sides of the hearth—me picking at Rudi's matted fur, her turning her rings over and over. The modest fire warms the space enough that the ache in my shoulder ebbs, and I drift, eyelids heavy.

Then—a knock.

A single, solid thud rattles the door.

I jolt upright, talwar in hand before I've even thought to draw it. Aisha grabs her bow and notches an arrow. Rudi stalks forward, hackles high, teeth bared.

I creep to the door. One glance from Aisha. I yank it open

and flatten against the wall, waiting for her to fire.

She doesn't.

Instead, her bow clatters to the ground.

I step out, blade raised—and stop cold.

Aisha rushes past me. 'Help me get him inside.'

'Alfie?' The word catches in my throat.

We haul him in, blood-slick and soaked through. A lightning flash shows the damage—his face gashed, one eye gone. His breath comes in shallow, wet groans.

I slam the door shut. Another flash. A figure stands in the gravel outside.

My blade lifts.

I don't need to look. Aisha's already armed again, her stance tense. We step out together into the storm.

The figure moves fast—hooded, cloaked, with a gait too fluid, too silent to be entirely human. Rudi barks.

'Wait,' Aisha says. Her bow lowers. 'It's Lina.'

I mimic her, blade still tight in my grip. The creature passes without a glance and kneels beside Alfie.

My expression must give me away, because Aisha answers before I can speak.

'She was his lover, long ago.'

Inside, Alfie lies stripped to the waist on the kitchen table. The wound in his chest is just as bad as his eye. Lina turns to Aisha—silent, asking—and Aisha nods once.

The fire spits and coughs, then dies. The room grows so cold that I brace my arms across my chest.

It—she—draws a blade, slices her wrist, and presses it to Alfie's lips.

I wince.

'What the hell is this?' I ask, though I can't look away.

Aisha doesn't flinch. 'We've been around longer than we

143

should've. The first time, it was a necessity. After that, it became survival.'

Even as she speaks, Alfie begins to change.

His colour returns. His chest rises. The gash closes, skin knitting itself like time moving in reverse. His ruined face begins to smooth, reshaping into something half-familiar.

It's over in seconds—faster than healing should ever be.

A chill prickles down my spine. This isn't magic. It's something colder. Something wrong.

And yet—somewhere beneath the revulsion—sits relief. And pity.

Aisha turns away as if ashamed. 'With our numbers dwindling, we found ourselves turning to her more and more.'

Alfie gasps, then groans. Alive again, if not entirely whole. The eye is gone. What's left is a pale scar and a trembling breath.

Aisha cuts a strip from her shawl and binds the socket gently.

Alfie sits up slowly, sucking in air like someone who nearly drowned.

'The twins,' he croaks. 'I lost them.'

Of the three of us, only Alfie manages to sleep. The dhampir —Lina—slipped away into the darkness the moment Alfie sat up to draw breath, like a shadow lost to the wind.

Aisha sits opposite me, head rested on her knuckles, eyes fixed on some blank spot on the wall.

I'm busy tracing the silver inlay of my blade with a finger, counting down the hours, minutes, and seconds until dawn arrives.

Alfie wakes with the sun, raising a hand to the hole

where his blue eye once lived, seeming to relive the blow that took it from him.

'What happened?' Aisha kneels with a bowl of warmed water and a cloth to clean around his eye socket. Her hands are sure, gentle. More than just the hands of a killer.

'They ambushed us.' He grimaces as she lifts the bandage from his head.

She takes hold of his hand as she cleans his eye, then lays the wet cloth over his face as she cleans a razor. 'How?'

Alfie waits for the cloth to be removed before responding, and Aisha sets about shaving his shabby beard.

'There was a bridge that had collapsed. Hard as we rode, we couldn't make up the time lost. Darkness fell, and they fell upon us.'

'And the twins?' She cuts away the beard, leaving only his moustache untouched.

'One moment we were side by side, *winning* the fight. Next thing, I'm fighting alone.' He gestures to his eye as Aisha dries his face. 'If not for Lina, I'd be dead.'

'Do you think the twins escaped?'

Aisha stands. Her voice drops. 'Alfie—did they?'

He doesn't meet her eyes. Just tightens the bandage and says, 'I didn't see.'

'I'll go to look for them then.' Aisha slips a shawl over her shoulders and grabs her bow.

'No.' Alfie groans and pushes himself up. 'If they died, they'll be gone with the sun. If they escaped, they'll come here.'

'Doesn't dhampir blood give you strength? Maybe they drank from her too, fought their way out?'

Alfie's face flushes red, and his gaze turns to me.

It's not like that,' Aisha says. 'We don't take from her—

145

we never could. When she offers, it's her choice. We only accept it when survival demands it.'

'Besides,' Alfie grumbles. 'The twins have never tasted blood.'

'But you have,' I say, more accusation than question. The idea unsettles me more than I want to admit. That Aisha—so full of fire and grace—has drank from a creature not quite dead.

She draws a slow breath before answering.

'Only when I was certain I'd met my end.'

She comes to me, takes my hand in hers, and turns it over as though reading my palm.

'We do what we must to stay in the fight.'

My stomach growls, sudden and sharp in the silence. It hits me then—how long it's been since I last ate. Since any of us did. The hunger is more than physical. It's fatigue in my bones, fog in my head, an ache I hadn't noticed until now.

I rise from beside the fire, stretching my legs and arms.

'Give me your bow,' I say, voice low. 'I'll get us something to eat. Then you can tell me how this all came to be.'

It doesn't take me long to bag a brace of squirrels, and soon enough, they're skinned and skewered cooking over a larger fire built in the lee of the house.

Droplets of fat bubble up from the legs and drip into the fire with a hiss, and I sit, waiting to learn if I've sided with heroes—or with monsters of a different kind.

'Vitala was the name given to the vampyre that plagued our village,' Aisha says, settling cross-legged with a handful of nuts. Her voice is quiet. 'Just one monster. That's all it took.'

She stares into the fire, her eyes somewhere far away.

'Seven long, painful nights, and the village was decimated. My people turned or torn apart. Their bodies blistered and burned in the light.'

I want to speak—say something that might soften the weight of it—but the words don't come.

'Three of us survived. Children. We fled into the forest and hid. Just three, from a village of hundreds.'

'Your family?' I ask, already knowing the answer.

Aisha shakes her head, eyes lost in the flames.

'Devel,' I say. 'I am sorry.'

'It was a long time ago,' she replies, forcing a small smile.

'How long?' I ask, remembering the gifts of the dhampir's blood.

They share a look, and Alfie gives a nod.

'Seventy-four years ago,' Aisha says, her eyes locked on mine now.

'No,' I say, shaking my head. 'That means—'

'I'm eighty-one years old,' she says. 'I've been doing this a long time.'

I glance at Alfie. He looks away

'I'm older.'

'How much older?'

'A lot older,' he growls, rubbing at the scar beneath his bandage.

The smell of roasted meat becomes too distracting, my contorted stomach too painful, so I lift the squirrels away from the flames and pass one to Alfie.

The flesh is charred, the meat stringy, but Devel it feels good to eat something.

'What happened to the vampyre in your village?' I ask. 'The Vitala?'

147

A flicker of a smile. 'We set a trap. We caught it. And we watched it burn.'

Alfie chuckles. 'Three children, tackling a vampyre and winning. Unheard of.'

'So, you met, how?'

'I was forced to live on the streets, begging, scrounging, thriving. I became a skilled pickpocket. Until one day, I stole from the wrong English soldier. Or the right one, I suppose.'

'You two started the Kresnik, then?'

Alfie laughs. 'The Kresnik have hunted vampyres for thousands of years—since the first monsters crawled out of the dark.'

'The original vampyre was so powerful that it took the order a century to bring her down,' Aisha continues. 'By that time, the vampyre disease had spread across the globe.'

Alfie spits a knuckle of gristle into the fire. 'Her bloodline grows stronger and darker each night. They call themselves the Carmillas now, in honour of the first.'

'Their queen, Manette, is as ruthless as she is monstrous,' Aisha says. 'We've been hunting her for as long as any of us can remember.'

'It's said she spent a thousand years as a slave,' Alfie adds.

'To a tribe of nomadic male vampyres that kept women as pets,' Aisha finishes.

Alfie chuckles. 'You can almost understand her rage.'


As the morning sun burns away all traces of the night's storm, I sit chewing the last of the meat with the knowledge that the people beside me are older than their skin, and wiser than their weariness.

Aisha stirs a pot of pine tea over the flames, the smell

recalling many nights hunting in the pine forests of the Tokaj Mountains with Dati.

And my thoughts turn to Maria and Luca. Still alive— because I have to believe they are.

My stomach churns. Not from the squirrel, or the smoke, or even the guilt.

From fear.

From love.

From the sickening thought that while I sit here learning the history of war, my family is living its consequence.

'I can't wait any longer,' I blurt. 'Not like this.'

'You're not in fighting shape,' Alfie grunts. 'I doubt you could even ride.'

The silence presses in. And then it hits me—sharp and cold.

What I could do.

What I must do.

'How do we get her back here—Lina?'

Aisha stops stirring. She shares a look with Alfie before responding.

'Why?'

I swallow hard. My mouth is dry, but my voice is steady.

'Because... I need her blood.'

The fire crackles. The birds have fallen quiet.

'It's the only way.'

Aisha doesn't answer at once. She just watches the flames lick at her pot of tea.

Then she nods—once.

'We'll send for her.'

# CHAPTER THIRTEEN

## *The Fire Before the Storm*

The fire crackles. No one speaks.

Then Aisha stands. Silent. Measured. She draws a knife from her belt and walks to the front of the house, the midday light casting long shadows across the gravel.

'What are you doing?' I ask, rising.

She doesn't answer at first. Just kneels in the dirt outside the door and slices her palm with the blade.

Blood wells up—thick, black-red in the sunlight. She holds her hand over the stones and lets it drip. Once. Twice. A third time.

Alfie curses under his breath. 'You're serious.'

I glance between them. 'This will summon her?'

'It'll summon something,' Alfie mutters, stepping out beside us. 'Could be her. Could be them. Blood carries far — and there are things out there hungrier than we are.'

Aisha closes her eyes. Whispers something in a language I don't know. The fire behind us pops. Rudi lifts his head and growls, low and uncertain.

'We have no other choice,' I say to both of them—or maybe just to myself.

Alfie doesn't argue. He just sinks back down beside the fire, and we wait.

Aisha binds her hand with a strip torn from the hem of her shawl, the blood already drying black at the edges. She says nothing. Neither does Alfie.

I try to sit, but my body won't let me rest. I walk the grounds, into the forgotten vineyards that surround it, as clouds gather above the mountains, and I whisper a quiet plea to Devi Daj—Mother Nature. *Let this all be over soon. Let Maria live through this night.*

Rudi follows me, tongue lolling, but even he keeps checking the horizon, sniffing the wind like it's turned foul.

Aisha remains by the fire, sharpening a silver dagger with long, even strokes.

Alfie watches me. Watches the horizon. Watches the sun crawl across the sky.

The scent of fear is everywhere now. Metal and smoke. Sweat and nerves.

And silence. Thick and pressing.

Twice, I think I see movement in the vineyard rows. Once, I raise my blade.

Nothing.

Time slows.

Afternoon bleeds into dusk.

The light thins. Shadows stretch long and spindled across the ground. The trees whisper with wind, but it's the wrong kind of wind—sharp, not cold. Like breath at the back of your neck.

I chew a few nuts gathered from the almond trees on the south side of the house, ignoring the bitterness of the skins.

'I don't like this,' Alfie mutters. 'Too quiet.'

'It always is,' Aisha says, her voice flat. Controlled.

I stand just outside the door, watching the sun sink behind the mountains like it's being swallowed whole. The sky bruises purple and ash.

I rub my arms. I'm not cold, but the hairs on my skin stand upright all the same.

Behind me, the blood has dried in the dirt, a dark stain against the stone threshold.

Still no sign of her.

Just the waiting.

The wind dies.

The air thickens.

Then, a flicker behind my eyes—something half-formed, half-felt. A wrongness pressing in.

And far beyond the rows of dead vines—something shifts.

I don't see it. Not really. But I *know*. Like how you know lightning is coming before the sky breaks.

Like how animals scatter before an earthquake.

Not a sound. Not a footstep. Just the sudden knowing.

Something's out there.

Coming.

Rudi growls, low and guttural. He stalks forward towards the vineyard rows—ears twitching, nose to the ground.

I follow his gaze.

Movement.

A shadow stumbles into the edge of the clearing. Then

another.

Shapes. Human—but barely.

'Hold,' Alfie murmurs, drawing his blade.

Aisha rises slowly, fingers tightening around her bow.

I step forward, breath locked in my throat.

Then I see them.

The twins.

One cradles the other—Renata dragging Jakub forward with a trembling arm hooked beneath his shoulder. Their cloaks are torn, soaked with blood and dirt. Faces barely visible beneath grime and matted hair.

I want to call out—but the words catch. Something's wrong.

'Easy,' Alfie mutters, not sheathing his weapon, but raising it.

I look at Aisha, and she has an arrow drawn.

'What's going on?' I ask.

Renata collapses forward with a choked cry. Jakub crumples with her, landing in a heap thirty paces from the house.

Aisha circles around them, silent steps, arrow ready to fly.

'Help him,' Renata croaks, kneeling beside her brother.

Aisha nods, bow still drawn, and Alfie goes to the twins.

I get a flask of water and rush towards them, but Aisha's voice stops me.

'Wait,' she calls. 'It wouldn't be the first time they used our own as weapons against us.'

Jakub looks up at me with strange, hollow eyes. And something shudders through me.

Alfie kneels and lifts Jakub's collar as I toss the flask to Renata.

'What did they do to you?' Alfie hisses.

He pulls up the sleeves of Jakub's cloak, as Renata lifts the flask to Jakub's lips.

'Shit.'

Bite marks on Jakub's wrist.

'He was bitten,' Renata says, followed by a dry sob.

The words hang there. Heavy.

Rudi whines beside me.

The wind picks up again—colder now. Almost expectant.

'And you?' Alfie asks, rising, armed.

Renata shakes her head, lifts her own sleeves.

I glance at the threshold where Aisha's blood still stains the stone.

Aisha says nothing. Just keeps her arrow trained on her friend, jaw tightening.

'He's fading,' Renata pleads.

She lets out a hollow gasp and lifts her brother's hand. 'He saved me. Kept me going when I wanted to give up.'

I can't watch, but I can't leave. 'What happened?'

She nods, slow and trembling. 'We were ambushed. Fought for as long as we could, be we were no match, so we ran through the night.'

I look to Aisha, to Alfie. Both grim. Both silent.

'We got separated,' Renata continues. 'I was lost, wandering the wilderness. It took a day to find him, but by then—'

She wipes her face on the back of her bruised hand. 'A single vampyre, not a Carmilla. A scavenger. I cut its fucking head off.'

A sound stops the conversation. A shift in the air. Something sharp and strange, like the way your breath catches when you know you're being watched.

Rudi growls again, louder this time.

The wind stills.

The air freezes.

The fire dies.

And then—she's there.

Lina.

She doesn't walk from the trees. Doesn't approach like a guest or ally. She is simply *there*—a shadow stepped forward, cut clean from the night itself.

Cloaked. Barefoot. Ageless.

Her eyes—those pale, sightless things—find Jakub first. Then me.

No one moves.

'He won't survive,' she says, her voice like water over stone.

'He can,' Renata insists. 'You've helped us before. Do it again.'

Lina looks to Aisha.

A silent exchange. A shared history. A boundary.

Aisha shakes her head, slow. 'It's too late. You know it. What comes next—'

Renata's face crumples. She presses her forehead to her brother's. Her shoulders quake.

Jakub's chest rises—shallow, thin.

I want to look away, but I can't.

Then Aisha kneels beside Renata, touches her shoulder.

'We don't let our own turn.'

'Please,' Renata whispers.

Aisha closes her eyes. Mouths a gentle prayer—God, grant him a gentle road.

Then she unsheathes her silver dagger.

Renata sobs but accepts the weapon as it is pressed into

her hand.

Her lips press to Jakub's forehead. A single breath. Then —

A flash of steel.

And silence.

Rudi whimpers and presses against my side.

Aisha and Alfie close their arms around Renata.

I sit back, hollow. Cold.

Then Lina turns to me.

'You asked for my blood.'

The moment freezes.

I nod.

'Why?' she asks.

I glance at the house. At Jakub's still form. At the silver-bladed warriors around me.

A dozen answers rise. Revenge. Fear. Duty. *Love.*

But all I say is:

'I can't afford to die. Not yet.'

'And what will you do with the strength I give you?'

'Take back what was stolen,' I whisper.

Lina studies me a moment longer. Then steps forward, silent as smoke.

She draws a knife. Cuts her wrist.

The scent hits me first—sharp and iron-sweet. Not foul. Not rotting.

Something old. Alive.

My stomach twists. Pulse stumbles.

My lips part.

She extends her arm.

I hesitate.

*Then drink.*

\* \* \*

The blood is so much colder than I expected.

My vision blurs as every wound in my body flares—then fades. Heat floods my limbs. My skin tightens over muscles that no longer tremble. The night sharpens—edges too crisp, colours too bright.

And Lina's gone.

The blood in my veins sings like steel drawn across a whetstone.

But we must wait out the night.

We must take care of our own.

We bury Jakub at first light, behind the house—beneath a cypress tree warped by wind and time. Aisha speaks a few words in a tongue I don't know. The cadence is soft, ancient. Final.

Renata kneels beside the shallow grave, shoulders hunched like she's carrying a century of grief.

Alfie stands behind her, jaw clenched so tight it might snap.

No one speaks. Even Rudi is still.

The earth is too soft. Or maybe our hands are just too tired.

Aisha and I take turns with the spade until the soil covers him.

No marker. No name.

Just a scar of turned earth in a world already too full of them.

I place my hand on the grave. Whisper something I can't quite name.

A wordless promise, maybe.

I'll make it matter.

Renata stays kneeling long after we rise. Silent. Hollow-eyed.

Then, finally, she lifts her head and says, 'He should've died with a sword in his hand.'

Aisha kneels beside her.

'He died trying to protect you,' she says. 'There's no greater end.'

Renata doesn't respond. But something in her shifts.

Her hands curl into fists. Knuckles white.

Behind us, the day refuses to wait.

'Let's end this.' My voice shakes—but it's not from weakness anymore.

Alfie straps on his sword.

Aisha strings her bow.

Renata rises from the grave with wildfire in her eyes.

And together, before the cypress, we swear a vow.

Not peace.

Not justice.

Vengeance.

And liberation.

# CHAPTER FOURTEEN

## *Beneath the Cypress*

'We've only one horse,' Renata says, turning a slow circle in front of the house.

'Lucky I've lost a little weight,' Alfie replies, touching a hand to his bandaged eye, a grin curling his mouth.

For the briefest moment, Renata smiles.

'We'll find more horses along the way,' Aisha says from the shadowed doorway. And then we set off.

The path ahead runs east to the Northroad—dusty, cracked, edged with weeds and leaning fences. No signs of life. No sounds but our boots crunching grit, the steady rhythm of Aisha's horse, and Rudi's soft panting beside us.

Alfie limps, stiff from the night before. Renata walks ahead, her pace relentless, like she's trying to outrun the ache in her chest. Aisha keeps watch from the saddle, eyes sweeping the horizon, hand never far from her dagger.

I walk in the middle. Not leading. Not following. Just there.

By midmorning, we crest a hill and spot a farmhouse nestled in a hollow below. A faint curl of smoke rises from its chimney. A handful of chickens peck at the dirt. A white horse stands tethered beneath a lean-to.

Renata says nothing, just draws her blade.

'Easy,' Alfie mutters. 'We're not bandits.'

'They've got a horse,' she says, jaw clenched.

'And maybe food,' I add, stomach already tightening at the thought.

'We'll ask for help,' Aisha says, leading the way.

We approach slowly, Rudi at the rear. A woman steps out onto the porch—grey-haired, sun-leathered, eyes sharp.

'We're not here for trouble,' Aisha says before the woman can speak.

She eyes us—four armed strangers, covered in dirt and blood-stained bandages, trailed by a wide-eyed dog—and gives a short nod.

'No trouble. But you'll need to trade.'

We walk away with a horse, two loaves of dense rye bread, and a promise not to return. Aisha's coin pouch is lighter, and one of our daggers is gone, traded. No one complains. We break open the bread, chew the thick crust in silence.

Alfie rides now, Renata behind him. I climb up with Aisha, eating as we move, the bread settling into my ribs like a slow balm.

Later, we find an abandoned stable with a swaybacked mare still tethered inside—alive, though half-starved. Aisha brushes its mane, whispers something in her language, and leads it out like it's always been hers.

I take the horse, rubbing its shoulder as I mount.

We pass the burned remains of a cottage. Only the stone hearth still stands—blackened, cracked. Rudi sniffs the ashes and whines. The air stinks of suffering.

'Keep moving,' Aisha says, without turning.

Close to midday, Gyor appears on a hilltop in the distance.

My stomach turns. We have to pass through to rejoin the Northroad, but I'd rather be anywhere else. Even the horse senses it—ears twitching, nostrils flaring.

'Daylight,' Aisha says, sensing my unease. 'We'll be fine.'

We climb the steep road to the town. Smoke and death cling to every surface. We move through the streets like shadows.

'No time to waste,' Alfie mutters. 'Keep moving.'

He's right. I want this place behind me. With a shared look, we press on.

Then we reach the square.

And stop.

The buzzing starts before we see anything. Low at first, then louder. Flies—too many. A sound too alive for a place this dead.

'Oh my god,' Aisha says, turning her face away.

I ride up beside her and nearly vomit.

Laid out on the stones—dozens of townsfolk. All of them dead.

My eyes find a figure spread out like a star—the priest— naked, flayed. A message carved in skin.

It's not Maria, I tell myself. But it could've been. Still could be.

Behind me, Renata's breath catches.

Then she lets out a strangled scream. She leaps from the

horse before Alfie can stop her and storms into the square, fists clenched, boots crunching glass and bone.

She grabs a broken piece of timber and hurls it across the stones. It crashes into the side of a fountain, breaking with a sharp crack.

'Fucking cowards,' she shouts, voice breaking. 'Slaughtering the weak? Flaying priests? This is depraved.'

She drops to her knees beside one of the bodies—an old woman, curled in death like she tried to shield someone.

'We should've been faster,' Renata spits.

'It's a warning,' she says, louder now. 'They're telling us something. Don't come any closer.'

I dismount, walk slowly to her side.

'No,' I whisper. 'They're afraid. They know we're closing in.'

She meets my gaze—eyes burning, red-rimmed, wide. Then she breathes out once.

I reach down to take her hand.

Slow. Shaky. She rises.

'She's right,' Alfie says, spurring his horse. 'Let's get these bastards.'

Aisha stays beside me as the others leave the square.

'Remember why you're here,' she says.

'I never stop thinking about it,' I reply.

As we pass the priest, I slow to a canter, place a hand over my heart, and whisper,

'*Dav opre.*'

My eyes linger on what remains of these brave people—those who dared to resist.

Then Rudi gives a soft yap behind me.

And I ride.

Out of the square.

Out of Gyor.

Out of the grip of everything this place tried to do to me.

An hour later, the monastery comes into view, looking down on us like a castle—and all I can think is that Maria is somewhere behind those walls. Alone. Afraid.

My stomach rises and falls like the road that brought us here. My forgotten heart kicks back to life at the thought of seeing her again. And Luca—my rock—what has he endured?

The monastery looks like a fortress. Great stone walls encircle it, with a tall tower at its heart. The basilica's terracotta roof gleams and vines cling to the whitewashed walls. Between us and it lies a dense woodland, circling the base of the hill like a living moat, rising up to brush the outer wall.

We dismount and lead the horses on foot into the trees. The sky disappears. So does the monastery.

'We can get right to the walls without leaving the forest,' Aisha says, hitching her horse to an oak. She feeds it an apple, then drops to one knee beside Rudi. Stroking his ears, she takes his head gently in her hands and whispers something I can't hear.

'She's good with animals,' Alfie tells me, noticing the look on my face.

Rudi blinks at Aisha with soft, trusting eyes.

She unrolls a leather bundle from the saddle. Silver-tipped arrows gleam among the tools inside, and another two of those exploding ones.

'They sleep during the day,' Aisha says, turning a silver dagger in her hand before strapping it to her ankle. 'but silver doesn't sleep, and it never hurts to be sure.'

I lift the talwar, admire the silver inlay.

'That blade's reduced more than one monster to dust.'

Renata unfurls something at her hip. A whip—short, thick, the end glinting with silver.

'Such strange weapons,' I murmur.

'My nagaika,' Renata tells me, menace flashing in her eyes. 'Modified for my particular… needs.'

'And these were a gift from friends in China,' Aisha says, tucking the arrows into her quiver.

'China? I've never heard of it.'

Aisha smirks. 'So much you don't know about the world.'

'Let's split up,' Alfie says, tucking a pistol into his coat, sabre at his hip. 'Nura, Aisha—you head that way. We'll circle from the other side.'

They vanish into the woods. Aisha bolts in the other direction.

I chase her—Rudi bounding through the undergrowth beside me. Aisha is fast, a blur of orange and leather weaving between trees, but I'm quick too. I'm no stranger to uneven ground and low branches.

The trees thin, and through the gaps I see it again—that white fortress, stark against the green. My heart pulls tight in my chest.

Aisha slows to a walk, then stops where there's a clear view of the monastery. She takes out a spyglass, squats low, and scans the wall.

'What do you see?' I whisper, crouching beside her.

She hands me the glass. At first, I see nothing. Then—a flicker of movement. A man in dark robes. Then another.

'Monks,' I mutter.

'Thralled,' she says. 'They keep guard during the day.'

She points to where the forest reaches the outer wall. 'That's our way in.'

I glance back. No sign of Alfie or Renata.

Aisha moves to the base of an oak and looks up into its high branches. 'This is the one.'

She climbs quickly, shimmying up the trunk to the first branch, then leaping and swinging higher like she was born for this. She looks down, hand extended.

I take it and haul myself onto the branch beside her.

She's already climbing again. Graceful. Effortless. I follow, scraping my arms and knuckles, doing my best to keep up.

The tree leans close to the wall near its top. I stop beside Aisha, breathless.

'I'll go first,' she says, and without hesitation she steps out onto a thick limb, balances—then leaps.

She slams into the wall, clings tight, and pulls herself over.

My heart stutters.

Her voice drifts down. 'Hurry!'

I inch along the branch. It bows beneath my weight. I suck in a breath and leap.

I hit the wall hard—pain blooming in my ribs—but I hang on, scraping stone. A hand grabs my wrist. Then another. Alfie.

He hauls me over the top. I land beside him, spitting blood from a split lip.

'Are you kidding me?' I rasp.

He grins. 'Brains over brawn. That's what the old man used to say.' He gestures to his right. 'Steps are that way.'

'Renata?' Aisha asks.

'She went round back.'

Aisha draws her dagger. 'Time to go. Stay quiet. Thralls aren't true vampyres, but the blood makes them strong and fast.'

She melts into the shadows.

Alfie gives me a nod. 'Go.'

I follow Aisha, sticking close to the inner wall as we search for a way into the basilica. We round a corner, and she pulls me into a darkened doorway.

'The tower,' she whispers.

I risk a glance. The tower stands off to the side—unfinished. Workers haul stones and hammer atop a wooden platform. Other voices echo from around the bend.

It takes everything not to cry out for Luca. Aisha gives me a look like she's reading my mind, then gently pushes the door open. We slip inside.

It's dark. The windows are shuttered from within. But we see what it is—a dormitory. Row after bloody row of children's beds. I draw my blade and creep towards the door at the far end, where a muffled voice drifts through.

We press to either side of the frame. Aisha raises a finger to her lips and twists the handle. Light slices through the crack. A woman's voice carries in, calm and chilling:

'...servitude and obedience...'

Aisha opens the door a sliver more and motions for me to look.

Inside, thirty desks. Thirty girls. At the front of the class stands a pale, hollow-eyed woman.

And there, near the front—Maria.

My legs nearly give out. My heart swells and shatters all at once. I want to run to her, shout her name. But my feet are rooted. My breath won't come.

Despite the hammering in my chest, something sick coils in my gut. I ease the door closed and turn to Aisha.

'We can't get them all out,' I whisper. Saying it aloud crushes me. Aisha's gaze drops.

'We're unseen,' she says. 'We slip away, regroup, come back with a plan. Together, we stand a chance.'

'Leave Maria behind?'

'Whatever they're doing here, the children are unharmed. For now.'

'No.' I shake my head, tears blurring everything. 'I can't leave her.'

'If we take her now, they'll lock this place down so tight we'll never get any of them out. Can you do that to these children? To their families?'

She presses a hand to my chest. 'Is that who you are?'

'I don't know who I am.'

'I do.' She brushes hair from my face. Her voice is steady. 'I saw the truth the moment we met. You hide it — under grief and guilt — but it's there.'

'What truth?' My voice breaks. 'I'm just a lost gypsy girl with no place in this world.'

'No. You're a light in the darkness. You are strength. Empathy. The future of the Kresnik. And one day they'll speak your name with fear.

I shake my head. 'There has to be a way.'

'There isn't. Not yet.' She grips my wrist, presses my hand to her heart. 'But I promise — we'll come back. For your family. For all of them.'

I wipe my face, swallow the lump in my throat. 'If we strike now, it's still daylight. We might —'

'You're fierce, Nura. But not that fierce. We'd die trying to rescue so many children.'

She pulls me gently between two bunks and sits. 'If we try now, maybe we die. Maybe those girls die. Or worse— never escape. Or you come with me. We know what we're up against. We can plan. Work together. Get stronger. Return with force enough to break this place wide open.'

I close my eyes and drift back to my father.

*Crouched at the edge of the forest, his hand in mine, pointing to a gnarled tree bent in the wind.*

*'See that tree out there, standing proud and solitary against the forces of nature. Does it look healthy?'*

*'No, Dati.'*

*'No, it's all knots and twisted branches. Ready to topple any day. But the roots of the forest are intertwined. They draw sustenance from the deep, even when the savage winter has stripped them bare. They support each other like a community, that's what makes them strong.'*

I blink the memory away, the weight of his words pressing against my chest.

Alone, I've twisted in the wind long enough. I'm not strong enough to face this storm alone.

But together...

'Okay.'

I choke back tears and swallow the lump in my throat.

'Let's go.'

Aisha leads me back through the dormitory. Past cots topped with heavy blankets folded into perfect squares. Lavender hangs thick in the air, masking the stench of piss and fear.

She cracks the door. The sound of men at work pours in —and with it, the flood of thoughts.

Luca. Where is he? How is he?

'This way,' Aisha whispers, tugging my arm. But I pull free.

'I need to know.'

Before she can stop me, I scurry towards the tower, pressing my back to the wall.

Aisha follows, her presence like a shadow at my heels. We reach the edge of the basilica and I peek around the corner.

Workers load stone and tools into baskets, which creak upward to the unfinished tower. Others hammer and haul their loads up.

None of them are Luca.

Aisha grabs my shoulder, urging me away, but I shake her off and study the window ledges of the basilica—low, climbable. Three levels. I wipe my palms, steal a glance at Aisha, and hoist myself onto the first.

She creeps ahead to keep watch, muttering, 'You're going to get us both killed.'

I don't answer. I lift myself onto the second ledge, one arm at a time, stronger than I should be. Scraping against the stone, I get a knee up and pull the rest of myself after.

I glance down. Aisha is scowling.

'I won't wait,' she warns.

'I have to know,' I whisper. 'Then we go.'

She disappears around the next corner but comes back moments later, watching grimly as I reach for the third ledge. My arms bleed against the rough stone, fingers ache. The window above creaks open—just as I grasp the ledge.

My grip slips.

I fall.

The ground rushes up—and I scream until my flailing hand snags the second ledge. Pain tears through me. My cheek scrapes stone. I look up.

A monk peers down, his face blank with alarm.

169

'Shit.'

'Intruders,' he shouts.

I let go. Drop the rest of the way. Hit the earth hard but land on my feet.

'Come on,' Aisha yells.

Armed monks come scrambling around the corner—thralled and fast. I draw my talwar as Aisha dances into their path, unravelling the cloth from the end of her bow, to reveal a curved blade. Then, she cuts through them in a blur, ribbons of red trailing like falling silk.

I follow, blade in hand.

'In here.'

Aisha yanks a door open. We sprint through the dormitory, into the classroom. Children leap from their desks, startled. A blur shoots past my face—then the teacher clutches her throat, staggers, and drops. An arrow through her neck.

The girls scream. Fear ripples through the room.

Then—'Mama!'

Maria breaks from her desk, races towards me. I catch her mid-run, crushing her to my chest. My heart swells. My throat closes.

'I found you.' We both cry. But behind the joy, panic sets in. I've fucked everything up.

'We need to move,' Aisha snaps, slapping my shoulder.

I lift Maria into my arms. Aisha wrenches her arrow from the woman's throat, kicks open another door, and we burst into a narrow passageway. Footsteps follow—other children spilling after us.

Doors line the corridor. One creaks open. A thrall lunges out. Aisha elbows him in the eye, then slices his throat before he hits the ground.

We reach a wide, arched door and shoulder through it into the basilica.

Candlelight flickers across the stone. Monks sit at the far end in hooded robes.

Above them, a window long ago bricked up glares down like a scar.

Maria clutches my hand. We scan the space—no crosses, no statues, no gods. Only cold stone and watching candles.

Children spill in behind us, pressing up at our backs.

The monks rise together, no words spoken.

I step in front of Maria, raise my talwar.

Aisha is already moving—slashing through the monks like they're made of paper. One charges me. I swing, blade catching in his gut—but he doesn't stop. Doesn't flinch. I shove, twist, wrench the blade free, but he keeps coming, until Aisha's glinting dagger bursts through his throat from behind. He gurgles, then drops.

More thralls flood in through the door we came used, trapping us.

My heart thunders. I clutch Maria tighter. 'I'm sorry,' I whisper. 'I'm so, so sorry.'

And then—I see him.

Luca limps into the basilica from behind the altar, flanked by a woman so beautiful it hurts to look at her. The air stills. The thralls freeze. A chill bleeds into the room.

Aisha lowers her bow. I do the same with my blade and hold Maria close.

'Manette,' Aisha hisses.

The woman ascends the altar like it's a throne. Luca follows, head bowed.

Without a word, she beckons.

A thralled monk approaches. Kneels.

Three other women enter behind her, draped in elegance, smiling like saints at a funeral.

The monk drops his robe. Naked. Pale. I keep my eyes on Luca, refusing to watch.

But I hear it.

The wet rip of flesh.

The sucking.

The blood.

The woman tears into his throat and drinks, blood painting her mouth and chin red. The monk doesn't cry out. Doesn't move. He kneels, offering everything.

Maria whimpers, buries her face into my side.

When the vampyre's done, she tosses the monk aside like rags.

I hold Maria tighter and wonder if any of us will still be breathing come nightfall.

Then she speaks—her voice smooth as smoke, cold as slate.

'Oh, how I hate to be disturbed during the wretched daytime.'

# CHAPTER FIFTEEN

*Beauty of the Undying*

The hall is so cold it hurts to breathe.

Behind the altar, the three vampyres watch us with amusement — smiles too wide, too still. And as the monk dies — twitching, blood pooling beneath him — they laugh.

Silken, cruel laughter, like music played on broken strings.

I cover Maria's face with my hand, shielding her from the horror, even though I know she's seen worse. My arms curl tighter around her trembling form.

I try to focus on Luca — his face pale, distant.

But something's wrong.

He stands just behind the vampyres, unmoving.

Still.

Too still.

My stomach clenches. I whisper his name in my head like

a prayer.

But his gaze doesn't find me.

He's looking straight ahead.

At nothing.

I'm shaking—from the cold, from the terror, from her stare.

I can feel Manette watching me.

Not just watching.

Probing.

Her will brushes mine, cool and commanding, like fingertips trailing across my thoughts. She presses into my mind with whispered temptation. Inviting me to drop my guard.

To listen.

To obey.

I tear my gaze away. Find Aisha instead.

She stands firm—jaw clenched, dagger tight in her hand, sneering at the vampyre like she's staring death in the eye and daring it closer.

Then Manette speaks—voice velvet and venom.

'Your friends have no option but death,' she says, tipping her head towards Aisha. 'But you, child, you have a place amongst us, should you wish to live.'

Her eyes slide to Maria.

'And little Maria shall come to no harm. Of course.'

My stomach churns.

She sees the flicker in my eyes and follows it—straight to Luca.

And she smiles.

Softly. Almost sweetly.

'Sadly, we do not permit men to join our... community,' she says, her voice dripping mock regret.

The others chuckle—low, dark, delighted. Their gazes fall to the monk's body at Manette's feet.

Then her gaze returns to me—bright with terrible kindness.

'You'd forget him soon enough. Imagine it—an eternal life with Maria by your side. No fear. No hunger. No pain. Your every desire fulfilled.'

I nearly sway. Her words wrap around me like warm silk.

But then Aisha's voice cuts through it—sharp, real.

'Don't let her in,' she snaps. 'Lock your mind.'

Manette's smile hardens.

'Bring me the other others.'

A thrall stomps across the chamber to a groaning door. My heartbeat hammers against my ribs.

Footsteps. Heavy. Struggling.

Two thralls drag Alfie into the hall bloodied and bruised, but alive. Behind them, held between another pair of guards, is Renata. Her lip is split—her eyes—fierce. No submission. Just fury.

'Come, come,' Manette purrs. 'Let them join us. Let them see how welcoming we can be.'

Alfie is shoved. Renata fights the thralls at her side, snarling.

'You've taken enough today. Let them go or pay the price,' Aisha growls.

She holds Manette's gaze and raises her bow.

'Now, now,' Manette says with feigned patience. 'No need for theatrics. You can't blame them for being caught. But I'll admit—' her smile curls like smoke '—I may have over promised on the hospitality.'

Without warning, she grabs Alfie by the wrist and snaps

his arm like a twig. Alfie screams. His knees give in, but she doesn't let him fall. Instead, she holds his weight by that broken, twisted arm.

'No.' Renata lurches forward—but the thralls hold her fast.

Manette doesn't even blink. Just smirks.

'Let them go.' Aisha shouts in fury, notching an arrow with trembling hands.

'Monsters,' I hiss.

Manette turns her cold gaze on me.

'Monster?' she echoes, mock-wounded. 'Darling, I am Manette. Premier of the Carmillas. Blood of the First. I am legacy. I am power.'

'Tell that to him,' I say, pointing at the dead priest.

Then, finally, Luca moves.

He steps forward.

My heart lifts—and sinks all at once.

His eyes meet mine—and they're empty.

No warmth.

No recognition.

No love.

Only obedience.

'Luca,' I shout.

He doesn't blink.

Just stands there.

Waiting.

'Luca, you are my fire.'

Manette watches me carefully, gauging whether I'll break.

'You see?' she says, gently. 'There is no sense in fighting.'

'You're the fucking devil,' I hiss.

Manette sighs. 'Tiring, this daylight,' she mutters, releasing Alfie with a thud and a groan. 'Join us, or die.'

The thralls snap to attention. Weapons drawn. The other vampyres step forward, elegant and deadly. One of them stands behind Alfie. Strokes his hair with a red smile painted across her ashen face.

'I'm going to flay your friend alive,' she says, waving lazily and smirking, 'like I did with the priest. Oh, he was a talker.'

Maria is silent now — too scared even to sob. But her grip on my arm is iron.

Her tears soak my sleeve.

'No,' I whisper. 'Not like this.'

Movement — too fast. One of them's about to strike.

This is it.

And still Luca does nothing.

Doesn't flinch.

Doesn't call out.

Doesn't protect his daughter.

Just stands there, dead-eyed.

Maria's hand finds mine.

'Don't, Mama,' she pleads. 'Don't give in.'

The world slows.

Sound drops into silence.

I take a deep breath.

Look around.

Thralls leaning forward — poised to kill.

Vampyres grinning, hunger in their eyes.

Luca, expressionless.

Gone.

Maria's eyes burn.

'Fight,' she says. 'Please.'

Aisha steps forward. Bow drawn.

Renata stirs. She meets my gaze. Nods.

Not broken then.

Heat rushes up my spine. A furnace in my chest.

I plant my feet. Raise my weapon.

And scream so loud that my lungs burn: 'Fight!'


Aisha lets her strange arrow fly, and it hisses through the air across the great hall.

It hits no thralls. No vampyres either.

Instead, the smoking projectile embeds itself in the rafters—fizzing, pulsing. A warning hung above the world.

For a heartbeat, everything stops. Heads tilt skyward. Time hangs still.

Then—chaos.

Two thralled monks surge forward, unfurling bladed leather straps. I step back, dragging Maria behind me. The whips snap through the air, slicing past my face.

I duck. Stumble. Swing wildly. Miss.

The vampyres do not move. They watch, idle and entertained. Manette, at the back of it all, looms like a glacier —silent, cold, inevitable.

The chill rolling off her children leeches into my skin, into my fingers, into my thoughts. I can barely hold the blade.

Beside me, Aisha moves like fire. A blur of steel and blood. She cuts down a thrall with merciless precision. Across the hall, Alfie fights towards us. Renata thrashes to break free.

'Nura,' Aisha yells. 'Brace yourself.'

I look up. The arrow.

Then—Boom.

The explosion punches through the hall. I'm hurled sideways, Maria clenched tight in my arms, crashing into a splintered pew. Light bursts behind my eyes. My ears ring like struck bells.

Smoke floods the basilica.

The whip-wielders vanish into the fog, but from the shadows, a brute lumbers forward, dragging a blade fit for a bear.

I cough. Drop to a crouch.

He lifts the sword high.

I rise with a roar, my talwar slashing an arc up through his gut. Flesh parts. Blood floods. He falls.

I take his throat before he finishes dying.

Two more thralls rush me. I stagger. Blow lands—then—

'Come on,' Alfie yells.

He grabs my collar and pulls.

'Come the fuck on!'

The smoke clears. A jagged hole yawns in the roof. The wall half collapsed. Sunlight spills in, cutting the hall in two. Dust glows gold in the beam.

A handful of thralls lie crushed beneath the fallen roof.

The vampyres hiss—trapped behind the sunlight, prowling like caged wolves.

All but Manette.

She stands unmoved. Smiling faintly. 'Enjoy your daylight,' she purrs. 'But remember… it never lasts.'

Then she turns and disappears into the shadows behind the altar.

I don't follow her with my eyes.

Because I'm staring at him.

Luca.

He's standing by the altar steps. Still. Straight-backed.

His hands hang limp at his sides.

A vampyre grips his shoulder. Another strokes his hair like a pet.

He doesn't flinch.

'Luca,' I shout.

He doesn't move.

I take a step towards him, blinking back the smoke. My heart pounds like a war drum.

'Luca!'

He looks at me.

And for a moment—just a moment—hope.

But there's nothing in his eyes.

Aisha sees. She fires.

A silver-tipped arrow streaks towards the vampyre touching him—fast, true.

And she catches it without blinking. Smiling, she pulls Luca back into the shadows, then hurls the arrow straight at me.

I dive, roll.

It whistles past my cheek, splintering the floorboards where my head was.

Aisha's at the breach. She grabs Maria, lifts her, pushes her out into the light.

'Go,' she shouts. 'Now!'

Renata fights her way clear—bleeding, limping, but alive.

'Nura.' Alfie carves down a thrall. 'Get out.'

I don't move.

I'm staring at Luca.

And he looks straight through me.

I feel myself collapsing. Giving in.

'Nura,' Alfie cries, and I jolt. 'Come on.'

He raises his pistol, levels it at Manette.

The room seems to freeze in that moment.

And then he squeezes the trigger and fury tears loose from his hand.

I duck.

Maria clamps her hands over her ears.

Alfie lips twist into a grin.

And one of the vampyres falls to her knees. A patch of almost black blood blooming on her shirt. The wound opening. Spreading into a chasm. Burning.

'Go. Go!' Alfie screams.

I turn, scrambling over bodies, pews, stone and flame. My lungs burn. Eyes sting.

At the breach, Aisha grabs my wrist—pulls me up into the sunlight.

A thrall seizes my ankle.

I swing my blade. Feel it connect. Flesh gives. Someone groans.

For a second, I pause. Just one.

I turn back.

Luca stands in the shadows, framed in fire and ruin.

'I'll come back,' I whisper. 'You're my fire.'

And then the light swallows me whole.


My feet hit the ground and I sink to my haunches, chest heaving. I can't breathe.

How can I leave him behind?

I scream Luca's name and scramble up again, hauling myself back to the wall. A face appears over the crumbling stone. Then another.

Maria cries out.

I drop, shielding her, as monks come spilling over the

wall—others rounding both sides of the building. Some are hulking brutes, muscle and rage—not what I'd expect from a monk—others are thin as famine, skin hanging from bone, their movements unnaturally fast.

Alfie drops a few with his sabre. Renata surges forward, her nagaika slashing in arcs of fury, driving the thralls back. But there must be a hundred of them. We won't last.

I kneel, pull Maria close. 'Are you hurt? Did they—'

She shakes her head. 'I'm fine, Mama.'

The monks advance, wary of Alfie's sabre and Renata's whip. I raise my talwar. Aisha draws her final exploding arrow.

We form a ring—Alfie, Aisha, Renata, and me—Maria in the centre.

This is it.

I press my hand to Maria's chest, feeling her heartbeat. My own aches with the weight of failure. I wasn't strong enough. I wasn't—

A blur cuts across the gravel.

I shake my head. Focus as children dart over the wall into the trees.

'We have to jump,' Aisha says, glancing over her shoulder.

She looses the arrow, and we run.

I leap from the wall, Maria clutched tight, and we slam into the tree—snapping branches as we crash downward. I wedge my elbow into a fork to stop our fall.

Pain tears through me. Wounds reopen. My scream is strangled in my throat.

Blood smears the bark as I slide down, legs wrapped tight around the trunk. Aisha lands like a cat, takes Maria from my arms. Alfie drops like stone. Renata crashes down with a grunt.

And then, the explosion above.

Ears ring. Dust blinds. Thralls fall.

Bodies rain from the wall—branches snap, bone cracks. One lands beside me—red-bearded, dazed, blood pouring down his nose.

'Run,' Aisha shouts, cutting one down.

I stagger, Maria crying in my arms. Then sprint.

The big thralls lumber after us. But the skinny ones— *Devel save us*—they fly. Three of them flank us, forcing us away from the clearing.

I set Maria down. 'Run, baby.'

They close in.

No time.

I lunge at the nearest monk, slashing for his throat. He slips aside—too fast. I thrust. Miss again.

Then he kicks me in the ribs, and I crumple.

Maria screams.

I spit blood, crawl upright. Aisha fights nearby—two monks circle her, dancing around her blade. Maria rushes to my side.

'I've got this,' I gasp. I set her by a tree.

He comes again.

I wait.

Slash—he dodges. Thrust—he twirls away. He grins, taunting me. Then he punches me in the chest and I hit the ground again, gasping.

My talwar is gone.

'Go, Maria,' I wheeze. 'Find the horses.'

She hesitates, eyes wide—but obeys. Off she runs, through the woods like we're playing hide-and-seek again.

Alfie crashes through the trees, scoops her up, vanishes

with her in his arms.

I push myself upright. Blood runs from my mouth. Forest air fills my lungs.

And suddenly, I remember the first time I slept alone in the woods.

I close my eyes. Remember what Dati taught me about focus.

Breathe.

He charges again.

I plant my feet.

Breathe deep.

Focus.

This time, when he launches himself at me, I see the kick coming and my blade meets his leg—sinks deep. Blood sprays. He screams.

I spin, yanking the blade free, and take his head in one swift movement.

Another comes. I parry, gut him. The third—dead before he understands the fight has changed.

I join Aisha—slash a thrall's spine. She finishes the second with a blow to the throat.

Then more charge.

But something's different now. Lina's blood? My gift? Rage? I don't know.

I cut them to ribbons.

When the last falls, I look to the clearing.

Maria and Alfie reach the horses—but their pursuers are right behind.

One thrall corners Maria.

I charge forward. Drive my blade through his back—out through his chest.

He jerks once, then drops.

Maria throws herself into my arms.

Then a snarl—a scream.

Rudi tears a thrall's throat out.

Alfie finishes another, his boot crushing the last breath from the man's lungs.

'Death's the only freedom a thrall ever gets,' he mutters.

Aisha and Renata emerge, bloodied, panting—but alive.

'Time to leave,' Aisha says, gripping my shoulder. 'Take my horse.'

I lift Maria onto the saddle, climb up behind her.

'Come on.'

Renata and Alfie mount the farm horse, two crying children in their arms. Aisha leaps onto the swayback.

'Where's Papa?' Maria asks, tearful. 'Are we leaving him?'

'No,' I whisper, pressing a kiss to her head. 'We'll get him back. I promise.'

And then we ride—away from the monastery, from the ruins of everything we failed to save—into the burning light of a world that will never be the same.

And behind us, the dark remembers.

# CHAPTER SIXTEEN

## *A Woman Monsters Fear*

Gore-soaked, we ride for a long time in silence, until we come to a fork in the path.

'I'll get them home safe,' Aisha tells Alfie. 'Put some distance between yourselves and the monastery. I'll find you.'

Alfie nods, passing the children over to her. 'Be careful.'

We ride through the day, my arms tight around Maria, my face buried in her hair. I try to hold on to the joy thrumming in my chest, but every time it begins to swell, something cold creeps in. Death flashes behind my eyes. The scent of blood clings to us all like a second skin.

And there's something else—*her*. Manette.

Like a gold coin buried in dirt, she gleams in the dark—a beautiful trap. Despite everything, I'm drawn to her. And despite the sun beating down on us, I feel her chill clinging to my skin. Beneath my skin.

And what I can't see is Luca. No matter how hard I try, he's only a stranger now. A silhouette beside her.

It makes me want to scream. To tear out my hair and—

'Mama, you're hurting me.'

It takes a breath for me to understand. I unclasp my hand from Maria's wrist and stroke her hair. 'Baby, I'm sorry.

'Perhaps we should stop a moment, take a drink?' Aisha reins in and slips from the saddle, before lifting the children down, the reins coiled around her wrist.

I follow, less gracefully, and lift Maria down.

'You're crying.' I wipe her cheeks with my thumb. 'I'm so sorry I hurt you.'

'No. I'm crying for Papa. When is he coming home?'

He won't be coming home—*not yet*. Not until I bleed for him. Not until I earn the strength to face what took him. Until I carve my way back to him through the dark. And even then... I don't know what I'll find.

Will he be the same? Will any of us?

But I have to believe.

Because belief is all I have left.

'Go play on the grass,' Aisha tells the children with a soft smile. 'Just a short break.'

'I don't think that's a good idea,' I say, nerves twitching.

'It's daytime,' she replies gently, crouching to scratch Rudi's ears. 'We'll keep watch.'

I draw Maria into a hug and whisper, 'We'll bring Papa back. Once you're safe.'

Maria nods and trundles into the field with the others, kicking at tufts of tall grass. Rudi stays close by her side.

'It will fade,' Aisha says quietly.

'What will?'

'The memory of what happened.'

She lifts my arm, turning it over. I hadn't even noticed the wound—deep, red, raw beneath the crease of my elbow. Blood trickles to the ground as she cleans and dresses it with care.

'Focus on her,' she says.

'And my husband?' My voice catches. 'Should I forget about him?'

Aisha takes my hand in hers and meets my gaze. She's about to say something about Luca, about forgetting—but doesn't.

Instead, she says, 'We should be on our way before dark.'

Our path curves down towards the river, skirting Gyor. *Devel* knows what horrors Maria has already seen, but I can't bear to set foot in that place again.

With each rise and fall of the horse's lope, I slip deeper into memory. Back to that basilica. Back to *her*.

Just the image of Manette in my mind makes my throat tighten. But I try to focus on the figure beside her—Luca. My heart clenches. My chest constricts.

And I remember the vampyres behind him. Prowling. Poised. Wolves waiting for the signal to kill.

They'll come for us. I know it. Maybe tonight.

'Do you think we could have saved him?' I ask.

'The past is behind us,' Aisha says. 'Focus on Maria. On the future.'

I press a kiss to the back of Maria's head. Breathe in her scent. Hold it.

Then, low, I whisper to Aisha, 'I have no future without him.'

'Passage to England can be arranged. You'll both be safe there.'

'Without Luca?'

Aisha looks up to the sky, to the fading light and the emerging stars.

'The Kresnik aren't strong enough to face the Carmillas head-on,' she says. 'But we'll pick them off. One by one. And the day will come when Luca is freed—one way or another.'

'One way or another,' I echo, my heart breaking further.

'You made the right choice,' she says.

'I'm tired, Mama,' Maria murmurs, collapsing into my arms and pretending to be asleep.

'I know, sweetie. But we need to keep moving.'

We ride into the night—Maria slumped against me, Aisha scanning the trees, bow in hand, and Rudi bringing up the rear. A cold wind slices through the forest.

We take a detour, winding into a wood I know by heart, until I see it—Dati's spear, still standing, buried in the earth like a promise.

I dismount. For a moment, I just look at it.

Then I pull it free.

And we ride on. The river whispers beside us. And though I brace for them—the vampyres never come.

We reach Mama's camp just after dawn. Rudi sprints ahead, barking as he weaves between tents. The elders huddle around a dying fire at the camp's heart. And there, looking up from the flames, is Mama.

Rudi bounds to her side. She strokes his head—and then her eyes lift. She sees Maria.

'Wake up, darling,' I whisper, brushing my hand along

Maria's cheek. 'You're home.'

Maria stirs, blinking sleep from her eyes as we descend the hill. 'Are we really home?'

I nod, smiling. She hugs me, and I hold her tight. Mama rises, comes to meet us, eyes shining with tears, and I pass Maria down to her. They embrace, sobbing. At last, I feel something like safety.

'Where's Luca?' Mama asks softly.

I shake my head, climbing down.

'Oh, baby.' She pulls me into her arms.

'Maria, go get some food,' I say, gently easing her away. She heads to the fire, Rudi close at her side. She knows she'll be safe now.

'This is my friend, Aisha,' I say. 'Without her, we wouldn't have made it back.'

Mama nods, then takes Aisha's hand and hugs her. 'Bless you, my dear.'

Then she looks down at the two silent children.

'They have no home, no family,' I say.

Mama glares up at me, and for a moment, I expect disdain, but instead she smiles.

'Then they're already half Romani,' she croaks.

We join the others by the fire. We eat. We talk. We watch Maria and the other children sleep.

'Mama,' I say at last. 'I have to ask you something.'

She turns, the look in her eyes already knowing. 'You want to go back for him?'

I nod. Tears fall freely now. 'I can't leave him there. I promised Maria.'

'From what you've told us, you have no hope against these creatures,' Vaida says.

'Not yet,' I reply. 'But to bring Luca back, I'll have to

become something I never imagined.

I'll learn to move through shadows.

To fight without hesitation.

To be the kind of woman that monsters fear.'

Mama's voice is barely a whisper. 'Can you come back from that?'

I don't answer.

'And Maria?' she asks.

'They'll be looking for us. She won't be safe with me.'

Her face hardens. For a moment, she says nothing.

Then she reaches for a blanket, tucking it gently around Maria's shoulders as the child sleeps, her head rested in Aisha's lap.

'You want to leave her behind?'

I hear the quiver in her voice—just for a second. I take her hand and place it in my lap.

'After Dati died, you raised me. Kept me fed, warm, safe. I never thanked you properly.'

Mama wipes her eyes. 'Thank you for saying it now.'

'I need you to protect her, like you once protected me.'

'How long will you be gone?'

'I don't know. But I do know she'll be safe here.'

'You should move again,' Aisha says softly. 'Or leave this land entirely.'

The elders exchange glances. Vaida speaks. 'They won't find us.'

Mama nods, swallowing hard. 'We'll keep her safe.'

'Promise me.'

Her jaw tightens, and she takes my hand. 'Whatever it takes, I promise.'

The next morning, I kneel by the horses, Maria's hands in mine.

'You are my heart,' I whisper, brushing the tears from her cheeks. 'Beating outside my body.'

'Bring Papa back,' she says, sniffling. 'Promise me.'

I nod and kiss her one last time. Mama pulls her gently away. I climb onto the saddle, Maria's tears still warm on my hands—my own streaming down my face.

I try to tell her I love her.

But she buries her face in Mama's dress.

And then I ride.

She runs after me—barefoot, crying, calling out.

I almost stop.

Almost turn the horse around.

But I don't.

Because love doesn't always stay.

Sometimes, it has to leave.

Sometimes, it has to fight.

'I'm sorry,' I whisper, though she's too far to hear. 'I'm so sorry, my love.'

I'll be back soon. That's what I told her. That's what I'm telling myself.

But the truth is, I have no idea how long I'll be gone. No idea what I'll become.

All I know is I can't endure another night like the last—filled with fear, soaked in helplessness. I won't live another day hoping darkness never finds us.

And I won't abandon Luca.

Her hands still cling to him.

And mine still ache for her throat.

The night is coming.

And this time, I'll be ready.

I will sweat blood.

I will breathe fury.

Until my name is carved into the heart of every vampyre that walks this world.

Let them come.

I'm not hiding anymore.

# THE DHAMPIR—VENGEANCE MANIFEST

*I believe it was rage—pure, relentless rage—that kept her soul from being consumed.*

# SERIES PAGE

DAYDREAMER
THE ORDER OF THE KRESNIK

DECEMBER 2025

# ABOUT THE AUTHOR

Rick Houghton writes stories that explore issues we all face, blending folklore, horror and science fiction. Whether dystopian cityscapes or the shadows of history, his characters face impossible choices in worlds that refuse to let them go.

He doesn't believe in fairytale endings—only characters with the will to carve their own fate.

Printed in Dunstable, United Kingdom

65166189R10119